Taylor's Trek to Love

Great Smoky Mountain Getaways

Elsie Davis

Sweet Romance Publishing

Sweet Romance Publishing

Sweetromancepublishing.com

PO Box 778

Liberty, NC 27298

Proverbs 29:25

Fear of man will prove to be a snare, but whoever trusts in the Lord is kept safe.

A special thank you to Josh Rogers for his aviation insights to help further my research.

Chapter One

♥

Taylor crawled out from under the belly of the plane, arching her back to loosen the muscles that were stiff from being stuck in an awkward position for too long. She pulled out the rag tucked into her front pant pocket and wiped her hands to remove the black grease and grime clinging to her skin.

Margo, her Piper Navajo Chieftain, was meticulously cared for, and always ready to fly at a moment's notice. The PA31 was an old twin-engine plane her father bought after retiring from the Air Force as a pilot. Fourteen years later, a heart condition put an end to his flying days, and he'd given the plane to Taylor. She'd kept the name Margo, loving the fact her father had not only given the aircraft her mother's nickname, but the tail number was their anniversary and her initials. It was a wonderful reminder of the love her parents shared. A love that survived the ups and the downs of their journey together over the years, including the trials associated with getting pregnant with Taylor. It was a love Taylor wanted for her own life, once upon a time.

The only problem, however, was that Taylor's driving need to keep the plane in tip-top shape took up extra time. Lots of extra time that ate away into any possibilities for a social life. Except it was a labor of love...one that wasn't simply because her father had been obsessed with the plane, treating it like a second child. She too, was a perfectionist and felt as though a well-maintained plane was a safer plane. Her pre-flight checklist was twice as long as most pilots, and her post-flight checklist wasn't much shorter. Which is the reason the plane showed no obvious signs of wear and was almost as shiny as the day her father bought it.

It was a glorious memory, one she recollected as though it were yesterday. Her father had circled the plane high above them, becoming one with the sky...like an eagle soaring the currents. And then the plane got bigger and bigger as it came closer to the ground, wheels out, touching down and racing across the hard-packed dirt-road runway. At six, Taylor's mixed emotions ranged between awe and fear, worried he wouldn't be able to stop the aircraft. And when it came to a standstill, the sight of her father exiting the plane, a broad smile on his face and holding out his arms, drove away all fear.

Her mother had taken her hand, the two of them racing to greet her father. *And that's when it happened.* Taylor's first ride in an airplane. A truly magical moment, filled with awe and wonder. She vowed right then and there, that one day she would be a pilot and fly around the world. Twenty years later, she experienced the same awe and wonder every time she flew.

Growing up, she learned her father was a war hero pilot, and the bronze star he proudly displayed in a shadowbox on the wall in the living room proved it. She loved and respected her father and all that he had done...saving lives at the top of the list. He was a man she aspired to be half as good as to prove herself worthy as his daughter.

Not many people owned a plane at the age of twenty, especially not someone who didn't even have a pilot's license. While in college, Taylor had started formal flying lessons, and was finally awarded her pilot's license. Another magical moment in her life, but one that hadn't come without issue. The framed photo proudly displayed on the mantle at home included her parents standing on either side of her, huge smiles on their faces. They were proud of her beyond belief, but then, they didn't know her darkest secret. A secret only her best friend Sandy knew about, and one that would remain buried in the past if Taylor could help it.

Now, at twenty-six years old, she flew the friendly skies of San Francisco as a charter pilot, but the flying around the world part still hadn't come true. Not that she was complaining. Every day, she did what she loved most. *Flying.*

Taylor traced her fingertips down the side of the smooth metal of the belly of the plane, making sure the fuselage was perfectly intact. She then continued toward the right wing, intent on inspecting the flaps, and all the critical operating parts used for controlling the plane.

"Hey, Taylor. Going home sometime tonight?" Jethro asked, joining her. The older man's thin gray hair and weathered skin showed his age, but it was also a reflection of the experience he brought to the company. Thirty years of knowledge, to be exact. Taylor also looked up to him for the kindness and generosity he had shown her since the first day she started piloting for the charter company.

"At some point. I'm almost finished. At least I got back tonight at a reasonable time. I might even get to bed early. It's been a long week." She glanced at her watch. "What about you? You're running late, it seems. Nancy won't appreciate you being late for your anniversary date," she teased, grinning.

The grooves across his forehead deepened as he shook his head. "Trust me, I know. But my people dawdled as though the private charter meant I was at their beck and call for the night. We left over an hour later than planned. But the customer is always right...or so they say."

"I'm sorry you got stuck with those clients. They do have a habit of doing just that. The company should change the billing policy to pilot time, not flight time. That would move some folks along a little faster." *Wishful thinking.*

"Never going to happen. Unfortunately, industry standards will always dictate policy. You know, you don't have to go over every inch of the plane...before and after every flight. It's excessive by the best of standards and why they have standardized checklists," he teased, folding the paperwork in his hands and stuffing it in his back pocket to be filed later.

"Yes, I do." She grinned. "I've told you before, it helps me sleep at night." Otherwise, she would lay awake and go over her personalized and more extensive checklist mentally, and then it would take her even longer to go over the pre-flight checks the next morning.

"I reckon we all have our quirks. Mine is trying to make the wife happy." He shot her a wink and then checked his watch. "She's picking me up in about five minutes. Our date includes dinner and dancing, so I'm hoping the dancing part will make up for being late."

"Nancy will forgive you for anything if you take her dancing. Good call. Happy golden anniversary to the both of you. Sounds like a night of fun planned." Taylor had nothing and no one to go home to. Her plane was her baby, so staying here in a way, helped keep her busy. Staring at four walls every night at home held little appeal.

Jethro nodded. "Thanks. By the way, did you ever put in the application at Alaskan Adventures that you mentioned a couple of weeks ago?"

"I took care of it this afternoon before my flight." Fear almost kept her from pressing the send button, but she simply closed her eyes, said a prayer, and hit send. Whether they would even consider her for the job was another story.

"Nice. Nothing like waiting to the last minute. I thought you said the deadline was midnight tonight." He pushed his glasses back and peered at her more closely, as if trying to read her mind.

"It is tonight, so I'm early." Taylor chuckled, trying not to let him see the fear in her eyes she knew would be reflected there. For two weeks, she worked on her application, wanting to send it, but afraid to at the same time. The chance to pilot for the Alaskan company was an exciting opportunity, but the challenge itself was overwhelming.

There was always the question...was she good enough?

"Keep me posted. They would be lucky to get you on their team, though I would miss you dearly. I've watched you over the past few years, and you're one of our top pilots." Jethro started toward the door, waving back at her, but she hadn't missed his eyes as they glistened from the light overhead. She'd miss him too, but they would always be friends. Of that, Taylor was certain. And it was a gigantic leap to think she would get an interview with the company, much less hired.

Her current job with Charters R' Us was comprised of flying regular routes and landing at airstrips she knew well. There wasn't much deviation to her schedule, just a changing sea of faces. The new position would be completely different. Most importantly, it was the very element of the unknown that almost kept her from applying. The fear factor was as strong as it had ever been, which is why the safety net of regularly scheduled flights suited her best. *Until now.*

Taylor smiled, although inwardly, a gut sinking feeling filled her. "Thanks for the vote of confidence. Goodnight," she called out after him before he reached the door.

Too bad she didn't have the same confidence in herself. Once upon a time it hadn't been that way, but that was before she'd crashed and burned in her first simulator test. A time when she would have given anything to walk away from flying, the humiliation and overwhelming sense of failure, a secret she'd kept hidden for so many years.

Sandy was tireless in her efforts to keep Taylor from quitting. But ultimately it was the obligation to her parents and her own deep-seated passion for flying the friendly skies that had kept her moving forward to get her pilot's license. From there, she added the medical certification that gave her an advantage to pilot some of the more specialized flights that required more extensive medical training and understanding of the needs of patients being transported.

Taylor spotted the lone security guard walking the premises, the man barely looking in her direction as he made the rounds. The massive hanger housed seven small charter aircraft besides her own plane. Flying Margo had been one contingency when she took the job. Not that she allowed anyone else to fly her plane, but she didn't fly any of the company planes either. It was a win/win with the company, as few pilots looking for employment would use their own aircraft...if they even *had* a plane.

After checking the wings, she moved to check the tail, making sure to inspect the rudder and stabilizer parts. She made a few notes on her checklist, then headed for the small office where she worked when she wasn't flying, ready to lock up for the night. Her cell phone rang, and she was surprised to see Sandy's name flash across the screen. Her best friend would normally still be working at this time of day. North Carolina was three hours ahead of Pacific time, and Sandy's hospital shifts ran twelve hours long. It was a grueling pace for even the most dedicated professional.

"Hey, there. Your timing is good. I just finished for the night. Did you take off early tonight or something?" Taylor asked.

"Or something. Don't you watch the weather news?" Sandy's tense comment had her instantly on alert.

"I saw you all were expecting a storm, but it's clear here, so I didn't give it much thought. Why, what's up?" The storm was a massive rain event, the best Taylor could tell. During the fall season, there were plenty of rainstorms that could dump inches of rain within hours. Flooding was typically the worst part of the sudden deluge.

"The storm was upgraded this afternoon, and we had several tornadoes spin off from earlier this evening. They ripped through the area unlike anything I've ever seen before. I mean, we see it on the news, like closer to the eastern coastal regions or across the Midwest, but rarely this far inland in North Carolina. Raleigh got a ton of rain. The hospital staff is on overload and will be for a quite some time, but I'm taking a quick break to grab a sandwich and wanted to call you." Sandy worked in the emergency room, though Taylor often wondered how she went back day after day. Her friend was dedicated to helping others in their hour of need, but the last few years had taken their toll.

"Wow. Sounds rough. You sound tired, but I'm glad you're okay. I'm sorry because I know that means your long night will be even longer."

"I'm guessing since you didn't know about the storm, you haven't heard from your parents either. The western part of the state was hit the hardest."

Taylor frowned, suddenly understanding the reason for her friend's call. Sandy was like a second daughter to Taylor's parents. Her friend often joked about being the adopted daughter seeing as she spent so much time at Smoky Mountain Hideaway, her parent's bed & breakfast. But surely the storm wouldn't have impacted Moonridge much. The small community was tucked in the mountainous region, somewhat protected. Usually, it was the snowstorms they worried about. Something that could bring the traffic in and out of the area to a standstill for weeks if there were avalanches or road damage.

She checked her phone notifications. "There are no missed calls or text messages, so I guess that's good. I'll call them and check in when I get home. Thanks for the heads up," Taylor added.

"That's good. I'm not sure where the tornadoes touched down, and I've not been able to search out the news and postings online. I was going to give your parents a call myself when I get off work, but I'm not sure when that will be and figured you would handle it."

"Absolutely."

"So, anything else new? I've got about three minutes before they're expecting me back in ER."

"Well, yes. You could say that," Taylor said, knowing her friend would be overjoyed with the news. Perhaps it was the pick me up she could use.

"Spill," Sandy said.

"I applied for the Alaskan Adventure's pilot position." Saying the words out loud made it more real. She let out a deep breath.

"You mean the job I think you're perfect for? I distinctly remember you telling me you had decided against it. Not that I agreed with your reasoning, mind you." Sandy knew her all too well and never missed a chance to set the record straight.

"I changed my mind. You were right. I shouldn't let my fear control me, even if it owns me." It would be a huge step forward...*if* she got the job.

"You let the situation own you. It's like you hide behind the fear curtain, afraid of what you'll see. You're an excellent pilot and I would trust you anytime. Anywhere." Her friend's confidence in her ability never wavered.

"Thanks, Sandy. We've been over this before. I just don't know. For that matter, neither do you. You know I failed my first simulator test and that's a big deal in my book because I don't like failure. I mean, I've passed every test and check ride since then, so there is that on the other side to balance things out. Which is a good thing, since I would lose my job and my license if I didn't pass. I just don't like the what-if scenario, knowing I folded under pressure once before." Every morning Taylor looked in the mirror and was reminded of the truth she sought to keep hidden. Except you couldn't hide the truth from yourself. *Or God.*

"It was your first test, and you were a student pilot. We are supposed to learn from our mistakes, not wallow in them." Sandy was right, of course.

"True. I didn't let fear stop me, so you should be happy I applied."

"I am proud of you. Think of the fun you will have flying in and out of remote wilderness areas, picking up passengers who have a wild sense of vacation entertainment. Not my cup of tea, as I much prefer the calm serenity of the beach and listening to the waves roll in."

Taylor agreed with her friend. "Me too."

When you have a remote wilderness area and add snow and ice, it became an adventure of its own. A cold, hard, demanding challenge for fishing, hiking, backpacking, or whatever else people wanted to do in the wilderness. But flying them in and out of the areas, that was a challenge on its own level. *And the reason she applied.*

Perhaps it would finally be what she needed to prove to herself and her father that she was an excellent pilot, worthy of her father's good name and reputation. A standard Taylor strived for, wanting to make him proud. "But don't forget, as a pilot's dream job...it will be highly competitive. I doubt I will get the position, but at least I can say I tried," Taylor added.

"That you can. Stop worrying about the past."

Taylor's phone buzzed, and she spotted her father's name on the screen. "Hey, my dad is calling in. I should take the call."

"Absolutely. Talk later."

Taylor switched to the incoming call. "Hey dad. I was just on the phone with Sandy and heard it got rough with the storms. Everything go okay with you and mom?"

"Actually, no," he muttered.

Chapter Two

♥

Her father's words caught Taylor off guard. "What happened? Are you both okay?" She loved her parents and being this far away was difficult, especially when something went wrong.

"We're both fine, mostly anyway. God kept us safe and that's what's most important," her father said, his voice low and solemn, as though he had the weight of the world on his shoulders.

Something was terribly wrong. She let out a deep breath, trying to quell the panicky feeling threatening to close her throat. "What's the not mostly part?" Taylor asked, waiting for the proverbial bomb to drop.

"Well, the thing is, the storm passed right through Moonridge. There's no easy way to break the news, but a tornado spun off and touched down on our property. The main lodge took a direct hit and some of the building collapsed. Your mother was in the great room and a beam landed on her. Again, praise God, she's fine. Other than a sprained ankle and a broken leg, that is." With each word, Taylor's grip tightened on the phone, her bloodless fingers going numb as the rest of her went into shock.

She had to remain calm and get the facts. *All the facts.* "Where is mom now? And what about you?"

"I'm good. Your mother is resting comfortably in the bedroom, courtesy of the pain relievers the doctors gave her. But we have a minor problem. Actually, it's a major problem and we really need your help, Taylor. I hate to ask, but we honestly don't have any other choice."

Her parents never asked for anything, so whatever they needed, she would take care of. *Honor thy father and mother.* For Taylor, it was more than that. Everything she had was because of them. "You know I'll do anything to help you. Just name it."

"We need you to come home and help us with the guests at the inn."

"Oh." Taylor tried to wrap her head around his request. Moonridge was a long way away and her life was here in San Francisco. This was a big ask, but for her parents...nothing was too much. "What did you have in mind?" Thoughts swirled in her head of everything such a request would entail.

"Like I said, the great room part of the main lodge has a lot of damage. And a few of the cabins are damaged as well. We've got to hire someone to fix the place and the insurance guy will be out here tomorrow. Most of the guests high tailed it out of here when the storm intensified, and we saw warnings posted about the potential path. However, we have a few who stuck it out. There's only a handful, but with your mother in a wheelchair and unable to help, I can't handle the place on my own. It's just too much. I'm sorry. We were hoping you could take some time off to help us. Maybe a couple of weeks. Three tops. We've never asked for anything, but we need you now."

"What's going on, Dad? Is there no one else to help?" She should have just said yes, but the reality of her life demanded she find out more. It wouldn't change her answer, but it would help her understand.

"Everyone around here is dealing with storm cleanup. And I've got to pay whoever does the repairs, which doesn't leave us much extra in the way of money. And with the annual Fall into Winter festival in early December, we can't afford to lose the income from the B&B. Things are tight, Taylor."

Her father never discussed money, so this was news to Taylor. The bed & breakfast had always done well, so she couldn't imagine what changed. "Of course, I'll come and help you both. I need to talk to my boss, but since I never take vacation, I'm sure he'll clear me for a couple of weeks."

Now wasn't the time to tell him about the job opportunity, but Taylor could only hope the interview process was weeks away. Telling him now would worry him that he was interfering with her career and future. Time enough to tell him later…if she got the job. Otherwise, it wouldn't matter. "And Dad, don't worry about anything. I'll be there tomorrow and help you find someone to do the repairs."

"I'm sure I can handle it. You just fly safe and come home, sweetheart. That's how you can help us most."

"I've heard all the stories about the unscrupulous contractors who prey on older folks after a storm. When I get there, I'll start vetting the companies in the area and make sure you don't get scammed."

"Just come home." It wasn't an agreement to wait, but then, it was a process that would take time. And by the time her father was ready to hire a contractor, Taylor would already be home.

Talk about a quick night...one made worse because even after Taylor finally laid down to rest, sleep evaded her. Luckily, her boss understood why she had to fly home on such short notice. Of course, there were a few added comments about making her take vacation time. Though her trip agenda wasn't what most people would include on their list of fun things to do.

There had been little choice in her late-night venue. Between calling her company's admin office to have them file a flight plan, and then making sure everything that needed to get done at the house was taken care of, there was precious little time for sleep. Things like mail holds, watering plants with a little extra to hold them over, and making sure the house was totally cleaned, and the dishes washed, dried, and put away. It was another one of her routines she never altered. It came with the territory of wanting things perfect.

Seriously, though...who wanted to come home to a dirty house?

Taylor drove to the small airport and parked in the space reserved for employees. At five AM, the airport activity buzz was on the rise in preparation for the day's flights. Her next hour was dedicated to going over the plane from top to bottom. *Again.*

The exhilaration of going airborne on a personal flight was dampened by the reason. The fact she didn't take vacations, and as a result, rarely went home, added a layer of guilt that was unavoidable. In fact, it had been almost two years since she'd been home for a visit. Something she kept planning to change but work always consumed her. Everything revolved around trying to prove she was good at what she did and that she deserved to be a pilot, contrary to what the instructor had scathingly said when she failed her first and fatal simulator test.

After finishing her pre-flight checklist, Taylor pushed back the hangar doors, her scheduled take-off time fast approaching. She signaled the tow vehicle she was ready to go, then climbed into the cockpit of the Piper. The guy in charge hooked the towbar to her aircraft and then gave the all-clear signal for the driver to pull her out of the building. Once the pushback tug disconnected and moved safely out of her way, Taylor started the engines and ran through another instrument panel check. Satisfied, she taxied down the runway and moved into position. Listening closely, she waited for the final *clear to takeoff* from the control tower. Her headset crackled to life, and with final clearance, Taylor increased the throttle and then eased the plane forward, pulling back on the yoke as she reached optimal speed. She was airborne within minutes and proceeded to climb to the designated cruising altitude of twenty-thousand feet. Relaxing a bit, rechecking the instrument panel. Only then could she allow herself the luxury of immersing herself in the beauty all around. Billowing white clouds. Blue sky that reminded her of a Texas bluebonnet. Far below, the satellite view of cities and mountains faded. The sun beat through the cockpit window, warming her.

Soaring amongst the clouds, she was at peace. Close to God, the quiet silence heavenly. It was a time Taylor loved to pray and give thanks for the blessings in her life. This morning, her prayers were centered on her parents and their situation.

Hours passed, giving her way too much time to think of the situation at home, unsure of what to expect. Worry wouldn't change anything, and she resorted to prayers for comfort. Forced to refuel at the Nashville County Airport, the stop would add about an hour to the trip, but it couldn't be helped. Cross country was a long distance and Tennessee was about as far as she would go without stopping.

After refueling, Taylor was back in the air as quickly as possible so as not to exceed her pilot flight time based on regulations. It would be close, and Taylor was a stickler for the rules, so she eased her cruising speed a notch higher. With each crow-fly mile, her tension increased, thinking of her mother and the inn, not to mention the financial difficulties her father hinted at. Taylor sensed her father wasn't telling her everything. Both parents still thought of her as their little girl, shielding her from the worries of life the best they could. If they only knew...even their little girl had her share of problems, no matter how she painted the picture.

Financially, they shouldn't have issues. Over the years, the business had grown and was lucrative. So, for her father to say they couldn't afford to hire extra help to cover her mother's downtime, left some serious questions. Were they getting too old to manage the inn on their own? If Taylor had been around more, would things be different? Layer upon layer of guilt filled her, robbing her of the peace she normally latched onto while flying.

The plane bounced, hitting an air pocket. All thoughts of home and her parents vanished as Taylor scanned the instrument panel, just to be sure all was operationally normal. Another jolt, this one causing her to sit up and pay more attention. The clouds had darkened against the dusky sky, and a knot of fear curled low in her stomach. She had crossed into the Great Smoky Mountains and wasn't far from Moonridge but would feel better if she was already home.

Ten more minutes. That's all she needed before the rains unloaded from the ominous, now almost black clouds. The weather station had shown she would fly right into the cold front, but Taylor had hoped to be on the ground before it turned ugly.

Minutes dragged on as she drew close to her destination. Taylor flipped the switch to lower her landing gear and made a pass over the B&B. Her stomach clenched tighter when she noticed the gaping hole at the side of the main house. Seeing was believing, and even in the twilight it looked awful. Thank goodness her mother was alive and would fully recover from her injuries. Just the thought of her mom being anywhere near the rubble as it fell was enough to ramp up her worry level into overload. The sooner she saw her parents, the better she would feel.

Taylor began her final descent and spotted an elk running across the open pasture. Poor thing was probably out for its evening meal, and she'd spooked the animal. Taylor did a flyby and turned back around, giving the elk time to move to safety. The sight made her smile. She loved the wildlife here, something she got little of in San Francisco. But then, even spotting an elk here in the Smokies was a rare treat.

As she set the plane down on the runway, she fought to keep the aircraft level and in a straight line; the crosswinds buffeting her as she bumped down the dirt path. The plane finally came to a standstill, and Taylor cut the engines. A truck lumbered down the road toward her, the headlights beaming bright and the taillights revealing a dusty trail swirling behind the vehicle.

Her father.

Taylor slid out of the cockpit and moved to open the door, lowering the steps, just as he reached the plane.

Her father held out his arms, and Taylor gratefully charged down the steps for one of his bear hugs. She hadn't realized how much she needed the embrace until she was there. Tears filled her eyes and trickled down her face.

It felt good to be home.

"Hi, sweetheart. I sure have missed your pretty face around here." He dropped a kiss on her forehead.

"Missed you, too, Dad," she said, hugging him a little tighter. "How's mom?"

"She's doing great. Grumbling because she can't do anything and her pain levels are still high, but manageable. The news you were coming home really perked her up." They drew apart.

"Never fear…I'm here. I'll make sure she's well taken care of and that she doesn't have to worry about the inn. She can consider this a two-week vacation of sorts."

"Doubt she'll see it that way. She's been bugging me to go somewhere…but there's just so much to do here. It's never ending."

His comment reflected her earlier line of thinking that the inn was getting to be too much for them. "Dad, you need to hire someone to help. You two aren't getting any younger and you deserve some vacation time. Isn't that why you worked hard all your life?" They needed to clear the air on this subject before they got to the house. Her father was the business minded part of the team and Taylor wanted straight answers.

"Well, that takes money...and we're not rich. Our vacations are right here on our own property when there aren't any guests in residence."

"I don't understand. I thought business was good."

"It was, at least it was until the new bed & breakfast resort opened in Davenport. They boast Great Smoky Mountain Railroad trips, and some nonsense with casino junkets. Those are draw cards we can't compete with."

"You never said a word. Surely there's something that can be done to keep your old clients coming back." Taylor was reeling from her father's outright admission they had money troubles, and the inn was struggling. Another layer of guilt weighed her down, knowing she was the reason they had taken out a second mortgage for her schooling.

Her father shrugged. "If there is, I'm not aware of it. We just don't know how to compete."

"You should have told me. I'll look at the situation while I'm here and see if there's anything I can suggest that might help. If you need money, just let me know."

"You can look all you want, but as for money, the answer is a resounding NO. Parents help their kids, not the other way around. And please, don't mention this to your mother. She gets so upset over the subject."

Taylor nodded, knowing a closed subject when she heard one. "Well, okay then. Let me grab my bags." She went back inside the plane, grabbed her belongings, and then headed back outside. It was sweet of her father to try and protect her mother.

"So how was your flight?" he asked, picking one of her suitcases up and grabbing another by the handle to pull it to the truck as she raised the steps to close the plane.

"Awesome. At least until I hit the Carolina border, and that front started kicking out some winds."

Her father smiled. "Piece of cake for you. I wasn't even worried when I saw that on the news. Would take more than that to scare my little girl." High praise from her father.

The man thought she could do no wrong in flying. She hoped he never found out the truth about her past failure, because Taylor was certain she couldn't bear the look of disappointment on his face. "We should get going if we don't want to get soaked."

"True enough," he said, putting her bags in the backseat of the quad cab.

"The place looks like it took a beating based on what I saw from above."

"It did at that." The lines of tension deepened on her father's face.

"First thing tomorrow, I'll start interviewing contractors for you. When did you say the insurance guy was due to arrive? And we need to get good pictures before anyone touches anything."

Her father's gaze darted her way as he parked in front of the inn. "The thing is, the insurance guy stopped by this morning and already took pictures. And we have already hired a contractor. Renovations by Design start work in the morning."

"Oh no, Dad. I told you to wait. Let's hope they don't have designs on your bank account. There are some money-hungry shysters out there waiting to take advantage of people after storms." One more problem she would have to fix...if it wasn't too late.

"I may be getting old, but I'm not stupid. And I've run this inn since the very beginning. Reckon I know what I'm doing." He grabbed her bags, and she was left to follow him inside.

"But Dad—"

"Let me be the parent and handle my own affairs. Sweetheart, we appreciate you coming to help run the place, but we don't need you to take over. We would never ask you to do that much for us. And we are grateful you could make it. You're long overdue for a visit, even if the circumstances aren't good."

Taylor didn't agree, but there wasn't much she could do about the situation now that he had already hired someone. "Well, okay then. Did you at least check the contractor's references? Did you already give the guy money?" Her father might not want her interference, but she wouldn't turn a blind eye.

"I did because he needed to pick up supplies." Her dad wasn't seemingly the least bit worried about the very valid issues she was bringing up, and paying for supplies ahead of time was a good way to kiss the money goodbye and the contractor never even show up.

Taylor shook her head as she pulled open the screen door to hold it for her father. "Well, don't give the guy another dime until you see the supplies and he's done some work. You'll be lucky if he shows up at all, but I'll say my prayers."

"He'll show. It's a local company from Tremont Bluffs and they have an excellent reputation. Trust me, Taylor, I know what I'm doing."

"Oh. Well, that's good." Taylor smiled. Maybe it would be all right after all. Local was good, because around these parts, everyone knew everyone. Or just about. "But mark my words, I'll be keeping a close eye on the guy."

Chapter Three

♥

THE SIGHT OF HER mother in a wheelchair, one leg in a boot and the other in a cast, was a harsh glimpse into the reality of the situation. It hit Taylor like a sucker punch to the gut. She rushed to her mother's side. "Mom, it's good to see you. Are you sure you're doing okay?" Taylor could have lost her, and the impact of the thought drove her to hang on a little longer. She breathed in the Lily of the Valley essence her mother wore every day. The scent she claimed was her signature perfume but was really a department store special.

"Sweetheart, it's so good to have you home," her mother said, tears welling in her eyes. "And yes, dear…I'm right as rain. God protected me and other than a couple of bum legs, I'm ready to get back to work."

"Slow down, Margaret. The doctor told you to take it easy. And with Taylor here, you can do just that. Why don't you go over to the sofa and do some knitting? I'll catch Taylor up and show her around to see the damage and get her set up in the Fox cabin. It's the closest one to the house that isn't damaged."

Her father only called her mother Margaret when he was upset or worried. Add to that the lines of tension on his face, Taylor knew her father was trying to hide his emotions. But to anyone who knew him well…he was failing.

"I don't want to knit. I want to see Taylor. But fine, go get her settled and then hurry back. It's not like you'll see much in the dark. Did you tell her the *umm*…contractor would start work tomorrow?" she asked, a sudden light in her eyes as she stumbled over the word.

"I did." Her father's solemn tone left Taylor to wonder what was going on between them.

Her mother's eyes glazed over, a gentle smile on her face. "Good. I'm glad that's settled."

There was nothing settling about it, but what was done, was done…seeing as her father had already given the contractor money. But if the guy tried to bamboozle her father, he would have Taylor to reckon with. And she was no pushover when it came to protecting her family.

Turning over onto her back, Taylor covered her head with the pillow to drown out the woodpecker tapping on the side of the cabin. It sounded like a jackhammer, reminding her of the Pileated Woodpeckers that fascinated her. Not so much at, she peeked out from under the pillow at the clock on the night table, at 7:10 in the morning.

"Go away," she said, groaning in frustration. As if by a miracle, the hammering noise stopped. *Thank you, Lord.* It was only four in the morning on the west coast, and she got to bed super late the night before last, so her exhaustion was no surprise. Today was another big day, and not one she wanted to handle with only five hours' sleep.

She started a mental checklist. A sign she wouldn't go back to sleep, but perhaps she could stay snuggled under the covers longer. Foremost, check on her mother. The need for reassurance was strong within Taylor, even after spending the evening with her mom. Her father had heated a plate of leftovers and since Taylor was famished, it all tasted amazing. They had talked and laughed as though her mother weren't in a wheelchair and almost killed.

This morning, Taylor wanted to survey the damage in better lighting and make a list, taking detailed photos along the way. Then she planned to talk to the insurance company and get approval to start work, making sure they were on the same page and covering the full cost of repairs. Hopefully, the new contractor was approved by the insurance company, or that could present problems of another nature. Her father had been premature in hiring the guy, but there was little to be done now that he'd already paid him quite a bit of money.

Also on the list...Taylor needed to find out how many guests were staying at the inn, and what she was expected to do for them for the next couple of weeks. It's not like she hadn't worked the B&B with her parents when she was younger, but Taylor fully expected this would be a bit more involved. And by the sounds of things, every client they had was valuable for the future of the inn.

The woodpecker started in again. Taylor groaned, but this time, she wasn't so lucky as the sound continued. So much for a peaceful morning to adjust to a new routine. She slid out of bed and made her way to the window, determined to have a word with the aviary menace. Turning the handle until the window was wide open, she gazed down from the cabin loft's second story vantage point. The pounding grew louder, and she shifted her attention toward the sound.

Except her woodpecker wasn't a bird at all. More like a man. *Construction worker menace was more like it.* Who started work this early in the morning? This called for a change-up in the order of her to-do list.

The positive of the situation made her slightly more agreeable. At least the guy had shown up to work.

Taylor dressed in jeans and a T-shirt and pulled on a sweatshirt to ward off the early morning chill. She slipped on a pair of sneakers and headed downstairs and out the door of the cabin, crossing the yard to the roped off area for repairs. She ducked under the barrier and headed straight for the guy hammering on a board, his broad back and athletic figure imposing and capable. But it didn't mean they could trust him. Her father may have hired the guy on the spot, but the man needed to know she could fire him just as quickly.

Taylor drew near and stopped. "Hey mister, do you know what time it is? This is a bed & breakfast and people don't always get up with the chickens." *Like her.*

The man stopped, turned to face her, his eyes wide with shock. It was the same instant Taylor recognized him. Sun or no sun rising on the horizon, she would know Randy Cornell anywhere. Her ex-boyfriend was that kind of guy. *Unforgettable.* Brown eyes that were like warm chocolate, a chiseled chin, and wavy thick hair that begged attention. Hair she'd run her hands through in an affectionate gesture hundreds of times.

Randy tossed his hammer down and made his way through the debris while another guy shoveled the mess into a heap. "Taylor," he nodded. "I didn't realize you were coming home." It was a statement, not a question.

"I wasn't exactly aware you would work here either. Seems my father was short on information when he told me he hired someone yesterday. This simply will not work, not if my parents expect me to stick around and help." Seeing him instantly brought back memories she had suppressed for quite some time. She didn't want to feel anything for the man standing in front of her, but it appeared she wouldn't get her wish. Not that he would ever know. Those days were long over.

"The past is in the past. I want to help your father and he needs me. I'm sure we can figure something out to stay out of each other's way." Tension radiated from every pore of his body.

Not that he had a right to it.

She may have been the one to break things off first after they graduated high school, but he was the one who had moved on before another full moon had passed. For two years they had been an item, but that didn't mean he had a difficult time moving on. Nor had he even tried to save their relationship. At eighteen, she had been naïve, but no more. "Easier said than done. How long do you think the repairs will take?"

Randy shrugged. "Couple of weeks, tops."

"Convenient how you should show up lightning quick on the heels of the storm," she said, regretting the words the instant they were out of her mouth. Almost like a shrew...a word she disliked because she'd been brought up differently. Yet here she was, judging Randy without so much as giving him an ounce of trust.

"Not that you care, but I respect your parents. When I heard the inn was severely damaged, I dropped everything to come over and offer my assistance. My motive was merely to stop others from taking advantage of them. I would think gratitude over attitude would be in order, but then, you never followed protocol when it came to emotions."

Taylor frowned. "What's that supposed to mean?" It was one thing to do the judging, but she didn't like the tides turned. More reason not to fall into the trap.

"You were in the same conversation I was when you dumped me with no regard for our relationship or feelings that existed between us. Feelings that deserved more than a phone-call dump. Call me old-fashioned, but that's not how things are done," Randy said, surprising her. He'd turned the entire conversation to the past after telling her it wouldn't get in the way.

"I did us both a favor, and you, of all people, know it. Let it go. We were young and naïve, and I was simply the one brave enough to admit a relationship wouldn't work long distance." And the one silly enough to go running back to ask for a do over when she realized her mistake. *At least he didn't know she had come back.*

Randy shook his head, then glanced over at his employee, then back at her. "This isn't getting us anywhere and I've got work to do. So, let's get back on track with the here and now. I've got a job to do. I'll stay out of your way…and you stay out of mine," he said, his voice much lower so as not to be overheard.

At least they agreed on something. "Fine. But I'd like you to show me the damage, and I'll need photos and estimates." If they kept things on a business level, surely, they could both get through the upcoming weeks without arguing all the time.

One eyebrow cocked upward, the scowl on his face clear to anyone who cared to notice. "It would seem you don't trust me. Not sure what I did to deserve your skepticism."

"I never said I didn't trust you, so don't go putting words into my mouth. It's for the insurance company, smart aleck." It was common sense, so Randy's comment proved to be a bit on the defensive side. The question was…why?

"Oh, sorry," he said. Except he didn't sound sorry.

"You should be. Especially for waking me up at the crack of dawn." Taylor rubbed her temples, hoping to ease the tension headache that had been building since she was forced out of bed. "I didn't sleep well, and my head hurts. Waking up to the sound of a jackhammer wasn't exactly a highlight after a sleepless night. Can't you start work at like nine or something? There are guests staying at the inn who would probably enjoy some peace as well."

Randy grinned, softening his features. "Won't work, Miss West Coast," he said, reminding her of his penchant for teasing.

It would be easy to fall for his effortless charm, but she knew better. "Why not?"

"Because this is a bed *and* breakfast. Breakfast is served from eight to nine, with coffee and pastries set out earlier. Which means you need to be up and have everything cooked and ready to serve before eight. I reckon you ought to be down in the kitchen no later than six...seven at the latest. And that's only if you prepped everything the night before. Just saying."

Taylor huffed. This was all a joke to him, but unfortunately, he was right. What in the world had she signed on for? "I'll talk to my mother. With any luck, longer days for you means you'll be done and out of here sooner."

"What about you? How long are you here for?" Randy asked.

"Just until my mother is up and able to get around again." Which appeared as though it wouldn't happen anytime soon.

"In a hurry? When I talked to your mother, she seemed a lot happier than compared to the conversation we had while she was waiting to be discharged from the hospital. Now I know why."

Leave it to Randy to make sure she knew he'd visited her mother. Was he trying to score points because she wasn't here when everything happened? "I have a job back home. You know…obligations. And I'm up for a new job and need to be on hand to interview. Let's just make these next couple of weeks easier on both of us so we can get back to our regularly scheduled lives."

"Only if we don't delve into the past. It's not my favorite subject."

Taylor nodded. "Fine. There's no point." And it would make it easier to keep any residual feelings she had for the man on lockdown. Even at the opposite ends of the spectrum, she was having a difficult time forgetting the past. They'd shared so much. Their hopes. Their dreams. Their hurts. Their fears. And he had been her first kiss. That was something a girl never forgot.

"True. And since your motto is here today, gone tomorrow...it makes everything easy. It's not like I relish another opportunity to have my heart broken, so you've got yourself a deal."

So much for not bringing up the past. Taylor bit back her retort, unwilling to engage in a battle of wills with Randy. The problem was, she still cared. A piece of her heart would always belong to him. He was the first and only guy she ever loved, but life had moved on. Her focus now was on getting the job in Alaska. She didn't have time for relationships, especially not one with an ex who broke her heart.

"Just show me the damages," Taylor said, her voice curt and businesslike. It was the only way she knew how to be with Randy. Everything else in between would only lead her heart back into a state of confusion. And the last time that happened, she'd regretted breaking it off with him and had come home to fix things. Except he had been out with another woman.

Fear caused her to break up with Randy. Fear caused her to fail the simulator test. And fear continued to drive her every decision. Including not letting her heart get stomped again. Failing that simulator test was her own fault, but she couldn't help but wonder if her lack of focus or ability to get everything right was because her brain had been far too emotionally traumatized by the situation with Randy.

Which is why she needed to stay far away from him.

Life was good. Possibly a new great job in the wings. And the last thing she needed was to let Randy mess with her head.

Again.

Chapter Four

❤

Scrambled eggs, toast, and fruit worked in a pinch yesterday, but wasn't exactly the caliber of breakfast the inn guests were expecting. Last night, Taylor had done the breakfast preparations and now all that was left was the finishing touches...and she was right on time.

"You're such a blessing to us, dear." Her mother reached out and laid a hand on Taylor's arm, stopping her as she rolled out the dough for the fresh buttery breakfast biscuits.

"You all have done so much for me...out of love. Now it's my turn to pay you back...with love," Taylor said, stifling a yawn into the crook of her elbow. Morning came too early and not even an eight o'clock bedtime seemed to help. The time zone change was part of it, but truth be told, she'd been exhausted for quite some time. Long, dedicated hours on the job had a way of doing that to a person.

"It's truly appreciated. But I must admit, it's hard for me to sit still and do nothing. The sooner I'm out of this wheelchair, the better."

"I couldn't agree more," Taylor said, dropping a kiss on her mother's cheek. The added benefit was that if her mother regained the ability to handle the guests, Taylor could go home. Timing was everything with the new job opportunity. "I'm curious about one thing, however," she said, watching her mother closely to gauge her reaction.

"What's that, dear?"

"Randy Cornell."

Her mother's cheeks instantly flushed a bright pink hue. There really wasn't even a need to ask anymore, but Taylor still wanted to hear the truth. "You remember that he and I dated in high school, right?"

"We do. But that was so long ago," her mother said, a dramatical lilt in her voice that hadn't been there before.

Taylor wasn't buying into the complacency façade. "Yes. True...but still. Why him? It's awkward at best and asking for trouble. We broke up for a reason, and nothing has changed."

"Except he's still a nice guy. And it's like you pointed out to your father, there are a lot of crooks that come out of the woodwork after a storm. Your dad knew that and so when Randy showed up to help...it was a simple decision. Hire someone we know and trust." Her mother had a valid point, but it's not like Randy was the only contractor in the county.

"If that's the case, why not tell me when we were talking about it?"

"I don't know why your father didn't tell you. I mean, I guess we suspected you might not approve. But if you don't still have feelings for each other...then there shouldn't be a problem. You don't, do you?"

"Absolutely not," Taylor declared. It was unnerving to realize that this time, it was *her* voice that had taken on the dramatical flair. She finished organizing the biscuits on the cookie sheet and stuck them in the oven and set the timer. "I hope you two aren't up to anything."

"What do you mean?" her mother asked, the lines of her forehead deepening as she tapped the side of her mouth.

Taylor shook her head. "Don't play innocent with me. You know exactly what I mean."

"We like Randy. End of story. I promise."

She didn't believe her mother, not for a second. Unfortunately, there was nothing she could do about the situation. Getting anyone else to help wouldn't be easy as everyone good would already have been hired. And there was some truth to her mother's words...they could trust Randy. Not that she had been quick to admit it when she first discovered him at the inn. But then, other emotions coursing through her veins played a role in quick judgement.

Taylor checked her phone. She was surprised to see an email from Alaskan Adventures. She hoped it would be weeks before they got back to her, but it would seem that wasn't the case. Perhaps this was only a simple thank you for applying. Opening the email, Taylor scanned the document, letting out a sigh of relief. It was more of an informational welcome. It seemed she was one of eight candidates under consideration. The Human Resources department was running initial background checks and would be in touch to set up interviews soon. Hopefully, she would be home before they called to schedule her.

"Anything important, dear?" her mother asked.

"I applied for a new job, and it looks like I'm one of the eight finalists."

Her mother smiled. "That's excellent news. What are you applying for?"

"An adventure charter pilot position for a company in Alaska. It would be far more challenging than what I'm doing now and would allow me to see new and exciting places."

"Does your father know? He would be so proud of you. That would be like the missions he flew in the military...treacherous conditions and all. Not the bullets being shot at you." She grinned.

"For sure. Nothing compares to the heroic deeds that daddy accomplished. He saved so many lives. But no, I haven't said a thing to him. There's no point unless I get the job." Taylor was proud of her father, even if it was a heavy load trying to follow in his footsteps.

"I see. Still, you should tell him. So would that mean you'll be moving to Alaska?"

Taylor nodded. "It would if I get the job."

Her mother's smile slipped a bit as she let out a deep sigh. "I see. I had rather hoped your next move would bring you closer to home instead of further."

"Mother, we've talked about this before. I need to go where the jobs are, and that are places I want to fly."

"I know, dear. But a mother can always hope and pray. I'll be right back. I want to freshen up before the guests arrive for breakfast. That was a great idea, setting up the dining room table in the living room yesterday. It solved a lot of problems. And hopefully, Randy has the great room fixed up in no time at all." Her mother pressed a button on the arm of her motorized wheelchair and whirred out of the kitchen.

Forty-five minutes later, they had everything ready. Her mother had seen to drizzling chocolate sauce and icing on some pastries, while Taylor heated the biscuits and removed the vegetable-egg quiche from the oven, cutting it into generous portions. The aromas filled the kitchen, and she was more than a little hungry when the first guest arrived for breakfast.

"Good morning, Mrs. Ludlow," Taylor said, giving her best happy smile in greeting.

The older woman smiled, her rosy cheeks and twinkling eyes proof she'd slept well and was in good spirits. "Good morning. It's going to be a beautiful day. Glad to see the rain finally move out. Give things a chance to dry out a bit."

Taylor nodded. "It certainly seems that way. Have a seat and I'll bring you some coffee and a pastry to get you started." She poured the coffee, pushing the cream and sugar dishes closer to Beatrice.

"Thank you. Thomas will be along shortly, so pour him a cup and bring his breakfast as well."

"Absolutely." Taylor poured the second cup of coffee.

"I love it here. My home away from home. How's your mother this morning?" Beatrice asked.

"She's doing great, all things considered. It would seem even a wheelchair couldn't slow her down or dampen her positive attitude. She should be here momentarily."

"Wonderful news. I've been so worried about her. Must have been a dreadful experience."

"Thank you, Mrs. Ludlow." The peel of the doorbell echoed down the hall. "Excuse me a minute." Taylor said, retreating from the living room, before heading down the hall to answer the door. She pulled it open, more than a little curious who would be visiting this early that wasn't a guest.

Taylor vaguely recognized the good-looking man. She searched her brain to come up with a name. "May I help you? Jack. Jack Tinsdale? Is that you?" she asked. He had certainly changed from the awkward kid she remembered.

"It is." Jack grinned, flashing his pearly whites. "Long time, no see, Taylor. I heard you were back in town and wanted to come see for myself. You are looking as lovely as ever."

His compliment caught her off guard. "Thank you. It would seem news travels fast in Moonridge."

He rewarded her with another broad smile. "I reckon, but then you're one of us, so it's not as surprising as one would think."

In high school, nothing would have linked her and Jack in the same group. It would seem time changed a lot of things. "So, what brings you to the inn this morning?"

"Well, seeing you is a bonus, but I'm making some personal house calls to check in on folks in the area after the storm. Our company likes to help wherever we can. It's always so difficult for some people to pick up the pieces after a storm rips through and does severe damage. Knowing who to trust can be quite daunting." It sounded rehearsed, except for the part of seeing her. His flattery had been unexpected, but it was sweet.

"So true. Who is your company?" she asked. If only her parents had waited, Taylor might not have been in the awkward situation with Randy.

Jack cocked his head to one side, as though listening. His smile faded. "Is that someone working on the property already? You can't be too careful who you hire, you know."

The hammering ceased to annoy Taylor until it was pointed out. "That's the same thing I told my dad. At least he hired an old family friend. Randy Cornell. I'm sure you remember him from high school."

Jack frowned. "Remember him? Of course, I do. We used to wrestle in high school, and he was always the coach's favorite. Guy had a knack for coming out on the winning side. Guess he pounced on the opportunity for work with your parents."

"Seems like it," Taylor said dryly. "Would you like to come in for coffee? I need to deliver breakfast to Mr. and Mrs. Ludlow, but then I can sit for a few minutes. I'm sorry you came out here for nothing."

Jack's sudden smile caught her off guard. It was like watching a stop light. *Green. Red. Green.* "I would love a cup of java and, even better, the chance to spend some time with you." He shot her a wink, giving Taylor the impression that he was flirting with her.

In high school, she once thought Jack had a crush on her, but then she had dated Randy and everyone else seemed to fade away. Jack was good looking, she supposed, but more traditionally so than Randy. His debonair handsome smile and chocolate eyes left women hanging on his every word. *Something Taylor knew firsthand.*

"I'll be right back." Taylor headed for the kitchen and picked up a tray, loading it with fresh fruit, two slices of quiche, and a couple of biscuits. After dropping it off to Mrs. Ludlow's table, she returned to the table where Jack sat waiting. She poured them both a cup of coffee.

"This is good. Thank you. It's a shame your folks were quick to bring Randy in for the repairs. There's only two of them doing the work, making it slow going. I can't imagine your parents can afford much downtime with the business. Clayton's, my company, is much larger, and I'm sure we could have done the repairs in less than a week."

Less than a week sounded perfect. It would all but guarantee Taylor was back in time for the interview. Unfortunately, the timing was all wrong. "Sorry. My parents contracted the repairs with Randy, so there's nothing that can be done about it now. Unless something goes wrong, of course." But it gave her the idea of talking to her parents about the possibility of hiring two contractors. Her dad mentioned money as an issue, but if two companies did the work, they would each only get a part of the total...not more. And time was of the essence.

Jack's smile had slipped to yellow, but then, like magic, it was back to green. It happened so fast she might have missed the accompanying scowl if she hadn't been paying attention.

"Well, then...with Randy tied up working on the inn, perhaps you and I could go out. You know, like on a date. That is, if you're not still with Randy," Jack said, testing the waters.

Talk about a one-eighty in conversation. "No, I'm not dating anyone, and thanks for the invitation. You know, I think it sounds like a wonderful idea." More than wonderful, because it would be the single best way to get Randy out of her head. And perhaps send her mother a direct message to butt out of her love life. *Not that she actually had one.*

"Great. I'll pick you up tomorrow...say noon? Perhaps a nice fall picnic would suit you." Jack polished off his coffee, rattling the cup on the saucer as he set it back down.

Taylor nodded. "That sounds sweet. How about I pack our lunches and then drive you to a lovely spot on our property. It will give us a chance to catch up. It's been years since I last saw you."

"I look forward to it. Got to run, but I'm already looking forward to tomorrow." Jack grinned as he stood.

"What's tomorrow?" Randy asked, stepping into the room. His expression darkened as he recognized Jack.

"We're—"

"Taylor has agreed to go on a picnic with me. A nice, quiet, get-to-know-you picnic." It was the self-satisfied look on Jack's face that gave Taylor pause. Had she been mistaken in her quick acceptance?

"I see. Make sure you have her home before dark. Wouldn't want to have to come looking for the two of you." Randy's tone was anything but nice.

The two men were acting like they were back in high school.

Was Randy jealous?

Taylor prided herself on being honest, especially with herself. She had to admit, the thought of Randy being jealous made her feel better, even though she knew it was wrong.

Chapter Five

♥

Jack would arrive any minute and Taylor wanted to be ready and waiting, hoping to avoid any questions about her outing.

"My, don't you look pretty. Where are you off to this afternoon all dressed up?" her mother asked, moving into the living room and parking the wheelchair by the front window.

So much for slipping out unnoticed. "I'm not exactly dressed up, but I am going on a picnic. I figured while I was home it would be nice to ride out to one of my favorite spots here on the property." Taylor had picked out her nicest pair of jeans, and the sea-blue sweater was warm and fuzzy, something she had chosen at a specialty shop in downtown San Francisco. She loved shopping in the open-air markets and finding unique clothes and novelty gifts to send home. Everything came with a heftier price tag, but every now and then it made her feel good to splurge.

Her mother smiled. "That sounds heavenly. Wish I could come with you, but since that wouldn't be feasible, perhaps you should ask Randy to go. He could use a break from the hard work he's been doing the past two days."

The ploy was obvious considering two days wasn't much and the fact they were supposed to be in a hurry to get the repairs done. "Too bad I already have a date." It wasn't the first time Taylor felt the need to rein in her mother's matchmaking attempts, and somehow, she felt it wouldn't be the last.

"Oh. With who?" Her mother's smile had rapidly turned into a frown.

"Jack Tinsdale." It wasn't really a date, but Taylor wasn't above using the word to further reinforce the request her mother butt out of her love life.

"Really?" The lines on her mother's forehead deepened. "I don't see you being interested in a guy like that. Too full of himself if you ask me," she huffed.

"Is your opinion based on high school, or has something more current occurred? It would seem to me he's doing very well for himself and doesn't deserve to have his past muddy up his future. In fact, I think you should hire his company to help with the repairs. Two companies would get the work done faster and in no time at all, the inn would run at full speed again."

"No. That would never work," she said, shaking her head to reinforce her refusal.

It was no more than Taylor expected, but worth a try. "Why not? It makes good sense to me," she added, keeping the conversation on the business end of things instead of the personal side her mother wanted to meddle in.

"We simply can't afford to hire extra people right now," her mother said, her voice dropping a notch as she peered at the door.

Who didn't she want to hear the conversation? Taylor didn't have much time before Jack arrived but needed answers. First, there was her father's reference to financial issues and now her mother's. How bad could things be? "I can help you pay whatever you need. And then when the insurance portion kicks in—"

"No. We don't need your money. We are managing. It's just been tough, what with all the maintenance needed. Mostly though, business dropped when the new B&B opened about forty minutes from here. It's closer to the airport and they offer access to different fun excursions. It's simply not something we can compete with."

It was the same thing her father mentioned, but surely there was more than enough business for two bed and breakfast places in the area. Coming from her mother, it sounded far more ominous than her father let on. "Why didn't you or dad say anything before this?"

Her mother let out a deep breath. "You're always so busy, dear. And a child shouldn't have to worry about her parents," she said, her eyes glistening with tears.

"You took care of me when I needed you. It's only right I take care of you. And I've put in for that new job in Alaska and the pay is nothing to sneeze at. I'll be able to afford a lot more than I can at the moment. Trust me. So, you see, that job is even more important now than I realized. I simply have to get it."

"You know your father…he's a proud man. We'll figure this out somehow. But don't tell him I mentioned any of this. He wouldn't like it one bit and I'm not up to dealing with a grizzly bear for the next couple of weeks."

Taylor nodded, though her father had spoken to her about it already. It was cute they were both trying to protect one another. "Fine. Dad did happen to mention the new B&B in Davenport. Let me check out your website and see if there's anything I can do to help recapture some of the lost business. I'm not a marketing expert, but maybe I can figure something out that will help." More like maybe her best friend could help. Sandy was more well-versed in computers and might offer some suggestions, having set up a few websites for friends. It was like Greek to Taylor with plugins, codes, and images. Especially now with the shift to videos. *No, thank you.*

"That's sweet of you, dear. Thank you. Do you really want to go on a picnic with Jack? He doesn't seem your type." Her mother brought the conversation right back to where they started, no matter how much Taylor had tried to steer it otherwise.

"I'm not sure I even know my type. Jack seemed rather nice when he stopped by yesterday. Nicer than I remember from our high school days. People grow up...mature. You always taught me not to judge people too quickly, so I'm giving him a chance." Taylor spotted Jack's Mercedez in front of the house, the bright red flashy car, hard to miss. "And speaking of Jack, he's here. I've got to run." She dropped a kiss on her mother's cheek and headed for the door, eager to be gone and end the discussion.

Jack slid out of the car and headed her way, his pearly whites brilliant with his winning smile. "Hey there. A woman who's on time...be still my heart," Jack said, patting his chest.

"As a pilot, it's a mandatory trait," Taylor said, shooting him a grin.

He reached for her hand and helped her down the step, a gesture she appreciated. "It's good to see you again. So where is this special picnic spot you're taking me? Or are we flying somewhere? Lunch in Charlotte would be super cool. Kind of like the lifestyles of the rich and famous," he teased.

And nothing that appealed to Taylor...not even in the slightest. "Driving, sorry. I rarely take friends flying for joy rides in my plane since I use it for business. Keeps the records cleaner for taxes." It was also an excellent policy to keep friends she rarely saw from coming out of the woodwork and hinting at free flights.

Jack shrugged. "Bummer. But it's all good if you and I are going somewhere alone where we can talk. I can't wait to hear what you've been up to all these years away from Moonridge."

He still hadn't let go of her hand. "That would be a quick conversation. I feel your life has been way more exciting. One can't help but wonder seeing as you're driving a Mercedes and dressed in a power suit." It was a big change from the scruffy, long-haired boy she remembered from high school.

"Life's been good to me. There's no doubt about it." Jack grinned. Something he did a lot.

"Let's take my dad's truck. He took the car into town and won't mind. Besides, I'm not sure the Mercedes is good for off-road cruising." Taylor chuckled.

Jack opened the driver's door for Taylor and helped her inside, his hand lingering on her shoulder a moment before he headed around the vehicle and slid into the passenger seat.

"Let's get this party started," Jack said, his good mood infectious, although his choice of words, not so much. It was the third time in as many minutes that he sounded like a high schooler with his coined phrases.

Taylor shoved aside the negative thought and shot him a smile. "There's a place by the creek that should be super nice, what with the recent rain and all. The water should be quite high and rushing downstream. I love to watch the water as it crashes against the rocks, and the twists and turns it takes as it heads toward the lake. It's an excellent place to observe any wildlife coming in for an afternoon drink. We may have to hike a short bit, so hopefully you don't mind," she added, dropping her gaze to his leather loafers.

"*Hmmm.* I don't know." Jack frowned, but only for an instant. "These are expensive shoes, but I reckon I can deal if you can. You're worth it, sweetheart."

"Thanks, I think." She laughed, trying to ease the awkwardness of his comment. It wasn't a *date* date. More of a friendly get together. Taylor wasn't sure Jack was on the same page.

They bumped along the dirt road, Jack holding on to the side roof handle for stability. "I'm used to smooth rides, so this takes some getting used to."

"We're almost there. So, tell me, what exactly do you do with your company? You don't act or dress like any construction worker I know."

"You could say I'm the brains behind the brawn. I was hired to beat out the competition and land contracts for the Clayton's. No brawn needed, but I am still buff. Don't let the office job fool you." Jack beamed, but his condescending tone rankled.

"I'll trust you on that score. What are you working on now?" Taylor asked, unwilling to get into a discussion about his muscle, or lack thereof. That would cross a line she didn't intend to cross.

"The historic renovation project in Moonridge. Whoever gets the contract for the first house by the town council will be the favored source for all the work that needs to be done as they try to revitalize the downtown area. Some nonsense about recreating the days gone by, but it's a lucrative contract and not one to scoff at. I figure it's their money to waste. I'm good at what I do, so I'm almost positive I'll be awarded the contract. It's just a matter of time."

Jack seemed to have a very high opinion of himself and his abilities. But then, perhaps he was entitled to, based on his success. "Who else is in the race for the project? Since you're a local, I would think you would have an advantage over any outsiders."

"You would think so, but there's another local construction company bidding on the job. Renovations by Design. Your friend, Randy, to be specific. The guy is in over his head on this one, but he was determined to put in a bid. And, of course, there are several others closer to the Asheville and Charlotte areas, but their prices will come in too high. Trust me, I know what I'm talking about."

Taylor noticed the *your friend* part of his answer, but refused to comment. More jealousy that she refused to step into the middle of, no matter how flattering. "Well, I'm sure they'll do a thorough investigation and pick the best company for the job. Good luck."

"Luck isn't needed. A campaign agenda works best in situations like this. Trust me, I know the drill, and it won't be the first time I've had to point out some serious flaws in the competition to the committee making the decision."

It sounded like a negative ad campaign, something Taylor wasn't overly fond of...especially when it seemed they were the only campaign strategies used nowadays. She found it all rather boring and preferred to judge the merit of a candidate on their skill level, what they offered, and how closely they aligned with what she envisioned. "Perhaps you should point out the skill level of your team of workers and some of the other projects you've done. Let your work speak for itself."

Jack shook his head. "Easier said than done, Taylor. People are never happy when they must foot the bill. But then, they lack an understanding of what needs to be done and the limited options available. They can't always have it their way."

"I see." She didn't, but it wasn't worth pushing the issue. It was a beautiful day, and she wanted to enjoy what little time she had off this afternoon. All too soon, they would need to return to the inn, and she would have to start dinner.

Taylor parked near one of her favorite spots and grabbed the backpack she'd tossed in the truck's bed, slinging it over her shoulder. "This way," she said, leading him down the narrow path. She shifted the backpack, as it was heavy from the jug of tea she was hauling. Taylor was tempted to ask Jack to carry it, but it seemed he was fixated on watching every step he took, not wanting to get his shoes dirty.

"Here we are," she said, dropping the pack and rolling her shoulders to work out the knots that had taken up residence.

Jack caught up, frowning as he inspected his shoes. "Oh well. Italian leather and mud don't mix. These will need to be thrown out."

She hated that he was more concerned with his shoes than the beauty all around. "But look around. Isn't this place amazing?"

"It's nice. In fact, I can envision a house right here. Better still, several houses if you wanted to develop the area. This would be a lucrative prospect, for sure. People love waterfront property. I could draw you up a proposal."

Taylor frowned. Jack's line of thinking was like dumping ice cold water over one's head. Nothing subtle or wanted. "No thanks. My folks aren't interested in selling or developing. I'd rather keep this place for myself." It was sad that Jack saw everything through dollar signs, missing the beauty and the magic of the area.

Perhaps bringing him out here was a mistake.

She unfolded the blanket and emptied the contents of the backpack. They sat down, side by side, Taylor making sure the sandwiches were strategically placed between them. "I hope you like ham and cheese. I also brought some cheese and crackers and fruit. Lots to choose from."

Jack shrugged. "It's passe for my taste, but I'm sure if you made the sandwiches, they'll be delicious." Talk about a double-edged sword compliment.

"Thanks...I think."

"What? I mean it. Ham and cheese sounds boring, but I'm sure you know what you're doing in the kitchen and have added some special touches to make them more exciting." His comment rankled, but the joke was on him.

Mustard and mayonnaise were the full extent of her culinary add-ons. Now, if one considered she only put mustard on the meat side and mayonnaise on the cheese side as culinary expertise, then he was spot on.

"Did you bring a bottle of champagne to go with the fruit?" he asked, leaning in and bumping shoulders with her.

More and more Taylor realized that even if Jack was a nice guy, they simply didn't match up for...well anything. "Sorry. There's nothing better than ice cold sweet tea on a picnic, so I brewed some this morning."

"White wine is also nice," Jack countered.

"I'm sure it can be, but I don't like to drink. I never know when I'll be called in to fly, and it's better if I don't." It was her own personal rule to live by, not that he would understand.

Jack's jaw dropped in disbelief. "Surely, you jest. You're on vacation. Live a little."

"It's okay, honestly. It's not that I never have something, it's just not a big deal to me." Once, while in her pilot's training, she saw the results of alcohol and the devastating effect it could have on a pilot. The guy claimed he only had a few, but when pulled for a drug and alcohol test before a flight…it had been at least one too many. And the end of his career.

Jack picked up a grape and popped one into his mouth. He picked up a second one, but held it out close to her lips, trying to feed her. Not to be rude, Taylor opened her mouth and took the grape, surprised when his fingers lingered on her lips.

Taylor pulled back. "Jack, you and I are just friends, right? I mean, I live in California. I'm not here to start anything, especially as it wouldn't make sense. I certainly didn't come on a picnic with you to give you the wrong idea."

She was mollified when Jack shook his head in agreement. "Totally on the same page. You're leaving. But while you're here, there's nothing to say we can't have fun together. I like you, Taylor. A lot. And I'm hoping you might feel the same way."

"Isn't that what this get-to-know you picnic is all about?" she asked, evading a direct answer to his question. Jack was saying one thing, and if she didn't miss her guess...he was meaning another. Taylor's faith had always held her in check...wanting more than a meaningless relationship. Love, marriage, family. *In that order.*

"Absolutely," he grinned.

They polished off the sandwiches and snacks, the conversation mostly centered on Jack. It would seem there was no shortage of information for him to share.

A large bird flew overhead, capturing her attention. "Look," she said, shielding her eyes to see better. Jack looked to her left in the direction she pointed, appearing interested. At last, they had something in common. Taylor lay back on the blanket, gazing up at the sky, making it easier to watch the hawk soar in the current.

A shadow fell on her face just as Jack leaned down...to kiss her. Taylor pushed him away and rolled to the side, coming to her feet. "Whoa. What was that for? I thought we were doing the friend thing?"

"Friends can kiss. You are just so irresistible. To be honest...I had a thing for you in high school. I know you never noticed me, but it doesn't change how I felt." He sounded so sincere; it diffused her reaction down to a simmer.

"I didn't know that. I'm sorry." An inkling perhaps, but not one that remotely held her interest when she was sixteen. But she also knew how much it hurt when someone didn't love you back the way you wanted.

"You only had eyes for Randy Cornell." Resentment echoed in his every word.

"True, but that changed. We are all older and wiser. Life has a way of putting things into perspective."

Jack's smile returned. "That's what I'm hoping for." It would seem he could bounce back with the best of them.

"But just friends...right?" she asked, needing reassurance. Jack seemed nice enough, but there wasn't an ounce of attraction toward him. Whether it was his childish phrases, or cocky attitude, or a little of both, she didn't know.

"Friends is an excellent start and more than I could have hoped for before you returned home."

For the next half hour, Taylor stayed on guard more, not willing to give Jack any opportunity to misread the situation and give him hope where there wasn't any. She may have only had eyes for Randy in high school but given the state of heart since her return home, some things never changed. Another good reason for her to leave Moonridge as soon as possible.

It was a matter of self-preservation.

Chapter Six

♥

TAYLOR DANCED AROUND THE kitchen to her favorite Christian music station while she prepped the crab and parmesan artichoke dip. Her father had picked up the ingredients while he was in town.

After cutting her not-so-great afternoon outing short, the rest of the evening would consist of good food and conversation, and the promise of an early bedtime. Jack had been nice enough, just full of himself. And he didn't like to be turned down by anyone. He hadn't taken her rejection of his invitation to go out again very well, but there was no way she wanted to sit through another hour of the man extolling his virtues.

Unfortunately, her early return had also played right into her mother's plotting and planning, her radiant smile of joy unmistakable before she turned and left the kitchen after grabbing a glass of iced tea.

Tonight's fireside gathering would be outdoors since the great room was out of commission, and with only five guests, there was time for a little extra pizazz in her preparations. Candles burned on the counter, filling the room with a vanilla scent that calmed her into a peaceful place. There wasn't much time back in the city for the simple pleasures of aromatherapy and food preparation. Life was more than living in the fast lane. She diced up the crab, unable to resist eating a few pieces, and savoring the sweet, mouth-watering flavor.

The plastic that hung between the kitchen and the great room suddenly crackled as it was pushed back. Randy scooted through the opening, dropping the plastic back in place to keep the dust and cold at bay from the rest of the house. A sudden rush of adrenaline swept away Taylor's peace and calm.

Leave it to Randy to be the one person who could have that effect on her.

"Nice to see you back so soon," Randy said, his affable grin mocking her.

Taylor rolled her eyes. "Let me guess...my mother told you. How nice." Her matchmaking mother was certainly not giving an inch to her daughter's request to butt out.

"Well, she stopped by and mentioned you were home." He snapped a carrot stick in two and popped half in his mouth, his lopsided grin irritating her further.

Taylor knew one way to wipe the silly smile off his face. "Call it an advanced warning, but you should know my mother has an agenda."

"Oh? How so?" Randy asked, still seemingly unconcerned.

"Are you that obtuse? Her agenda is you and me. As in together again." The words didn't sound so awful coming out of her mouth, a sure sign she was playing with fire. Having Randy around was messing with her head…and her heart.

Randy shook his head, his gaze steadfast on her. "Why would your mother care about us? I mean, she just stopped by to bring me some sweet tea. That's not exactly an agenda. I think you're overreacting. Wouldn't be the first time."

So much for a truce. "Talk about a cheap shot. The problem is my mother has always liked you. Don't you think it's a little too coincidental that we suddenly both happen to be here at the same time?"

Randy chuckled. "That's the result of a storm…not your mother. So okay, maybe in a roundabout way, but not really. Don't overthink it. There's nothing between us and we both know that."

"I'm not even sure what you meant by the first part, but I agree on the second. Still, I think she's taking advantage of a situation, and I don't particularly care for her meddling."

"We aren't the same silly kids pretending at love like we did before. I think we can handle this. Don't you? She's having a tough go of it right now. Maybe the idea of us together is keeping her entertained."

Pretending. An ugly word for what she once thought they had. For her, it was the real thing...until it wasn't. "All true. And given that I put in for a new job that would take me to Alaska, something my mother knows, you might be right. Simple entertainment at our expense."

"What's the job?"

"They hire pilots to fly charter clients into some of the more remote areas of Alaska. Some for retreats, hiking, fishing, climbing. You name it...they provide it."

"Wow. That sounds like an amazing job opportunity. You always were the adventurous type," Randy said, the smile in his eyes as sincere as the one on his face.

"What happened to you? It's obvious you moved back to the area, which is surprising given you went to college for business marketing and a dream to be a part of corporate America."

"Turns out, I'm a simple guy with simple needs. A home. A job I enjoy. A church family. And one day, if I'm lucky, a family of my own. It's all about being around people and places I know. I realized pretty quick that the city wasn't for me. I dropped out of college and did some on-the-job training for construction and repairs right here where I grew up. And it's turned out well. I went into business a few years back and things are picking up."

All of this was news to Taylor. More surprising than anything. Randy's view on life had experienced a whirlwind change from when they first started talking of hopes and dreams as kids. "I never knew you dropped out."

"It's nothing I wanted to sky write." Randy winked, his pilot's insider joke finding its mark. "I took some evening classes and eventually got my associate degree in home repairs and renovations. Looks better on my resume when trying to prove my competency." He shot her a wink.

It would seem there was a lot she didn't know about the man standing in front of her. But there was also a lot she knew. Most of which, once upon a time, she liked, probably still did. But she couldn't get past his defection, even if they broke up. "It seems you've done well for yourself. Don't you have work to do?" she asked, hoping he would take the hint. They were talking like friends, and it was stirring up feelings she didn't want stirred.

"I came in to get a glass of water."

"I thought you just had a glass of tea personally delivered," she said, calling him out on the inconsistency of his story.

"She offered. I didn't say I accepted."

"*Hmmpphh*." Taylor nodded as she pulled a glass out of the cupboard, filled it, and handed it to Randy.

"Thanks," he said, taking a sip.

"How are the repairs coming? I mean, you mentioned a couple of weeks, but any chance they will be finished earlier than that?" Jack had mentioned a bigger company would have it done in days, leaving her curious just how long it would take for two guys. Seemed like a slow process, judging from what she'd seen done...or not done so far.

"Everything is on schedule, and the repairs will be finished when they're finished. Your mother is having me incorporate some historical changes to the property and they take longer to implement. And any project I take on I consider it my duty to do my absolute best and that means not cutting corners. Quality over quantity." Under normal circumstances, Taylor would agree. Okay, so that wasn't true either. Under all circumstances, she agreed. "Can't you hire someone in to help speed up things for just this job? I really need to get back to San Francisco in case I get the interview."

"It's a step-by-step process. Everything must be done in a certain order to keep the project site safe. You can't just jump in and start tearing things apart. It could cause more damage, not to mention, be dangerous. And you're forgetting, your reason for being here is as much about your mother getting back on her feet as it is for me to finish the repairs before the winter festival. Not to mention, it's a contracted rate. I can't suddenly add in more expense."

Taylor shook her head, knowing his logic far outweighed her own. "Why do you always have to be right?"

"It's called honesty. Maybe you won't get the interview and you're worrying about nothing. Not that I wish that scenario on you...just pointing it out."

"Gee, thanks." Taylor rolled her eyes. "For your information, I already have an email that said I made it through to the interview round provided my background check comes through clean. And we both know that's not a problem."

"Well then, little Miss Got to Fly…maybe you could lend a hand on your free time." Randy finished the water and put the glass in the dishwasher.

"I'm already…oh, wait…you don't mean help you, do you? As in with the repairs?" It wasn't a bad idea. And she was handy with tools from working on her plane. How hard could it be to work on the house? Might even be fun…if it didn't mean working with her ex-boyfriend. But if she wanted to get things done and fly home, it might be just what needed to happen.

Randy nodded, the grin on his face more than revealing. "It was a joke. You don't know the first thing about construction and home repair."

A joke at her expense, but Taylor wasn't about to be put off. "It's a great idea," she insisted.

"No, it's a bad idea. A joke." Randy shook his head and started for the plastic barrier.

"You said yourself it would make things go faster," she said, following him.

He stopped and turned back to her. "Or slow them down."

"Surely you can teach me what I need to know. I mean, how hard is it to wield a hammer?" Taylor laughed. The more she thought about it, the more it sounded like the best answer to get her out of here sooner. "I know how to fix my plane, so it's not like I'm afraid to get dirty or that I don't understand the mechanics of things. Come on, Randy. You know it's a great idea."

He let out a deep breath. "The work is physically demanding and challenging. If you promise to do what I tell you, I guess it won't hurt. I can't pay you because you can't be an employee. My insurance won't cover you, so understand you are chipping in on your parents' behalf. Other than that, just don't make me regret my decision." He ran a hand through his curly, thick hair as though he already regretted the decision.

They skirted under the plastic tarp, coming to a standstill next to the man who worked with Randy. A quiet sort of guy Taylor hadn't even met yet.

"Dane Prince. Meet Taylor Thompson. Our client's daughter. She's going to help around here. She has an agenda to speed things up so she can get back to San Francisco."

"Nice to meet you, Taylor." Dane offered his hand, his grip surprisingly strong. The guy was cute, friendly, and confident. What was there not to like?

"Thanks. You, too."

"Enough of the frivolities. Let's get back to work. The bosses' daughter is keeping tabs on us," Randy interjected.

"I'm not here—"

"Relax. I'm teasing. Once upon a time, you used to like my jokes," Randy said as Dane turned and headed back to the wall he was working on.

Taylor leveled Randy with her gaze. "Once upon a time, I thought you loved me, so I guess we're even."

His smile disappeared. He walked to the wall and grabbed a shovel and broom, handing them to her. "These are for you. I need all the debris scooted into one big pile we can haul out of here."

Taylor crossed the line with her dig, and Randy wasn't happy about it. The easy camaraderie of moments ago had vanished in a split second. Taylor couldn't help wanting it back. "So, what changes are you trying to incorporate into the inn?"

Randy remained silent for a few seconds. "I want to make a few renovation changes that incorporate the history of Moonridge, you know, like adding a tribute to the Smoky Mountains and the old timers who helped forge the area. Things as simple as changing out the mantels on the fireplace and building a stone façade, more intricate moldings, finding the right chandelier. Even the paint colors must be more subtle to match the look and feel of the past without looking outdated. Your mother mentioned business has been dropping off after the new B&B opened. She wants to find some sort of special appeal that would make guests choose to come here instead."

"Interesting. She mentioned the same problem to me, but not that she was actively working to change things up."

"We talked about it, and I agreed with her suggestion. Especially since Moonridge has been moving toward more historical preservation. It's like a compliment to the community. As a history buff, this appeals to me. Not to mention, it will go a long way to show the town council what I can do and perhaps give me the edge. I need to be awarded the historical renovation contract for the downtown area. It would give the chance to expand my company, as it would be a huge undertaking and take years to complete the vision the town has for growth and attracting new business." Randy's passion for his vision was clear in every word. *Unlike Jack's.*

"I heard you were competing for the historical project in town. It sounds like an amazing opportunity for you."

Randy frowned. "Let me guess...Jack clued you in. Did he tell you he's after the contract as well?"

"Yes. I'm sure you're both very good at what you do, and the town council will make the best decision for what they need." Part of her wanted Randy to get the contract, but a part of her, the place deep in her heart where she hurt from their breakup, well, that place wanted him to lose. It was stupid...and selfish. And wrong. There was nothing Christian in the wayward thought.

"Just because he's local doesn't mean his company is. I highly doubt Clayton's would ever understand the complexity of the history of Moonridge and what it means to the people in this town." Randy's scowl had intensified.

There was no love lost between the two men, and Taylor was realizing it wasn't a simple matter of jealousy. "Well, okay then. I guess that's for the town council to decide."

"Time to get to work." Taylor was more than ready to chip in and help. Better than crossing swords with Randy. And anything that got her back to California sooner...she was all in. Because there was no telling what the charter company would do if Taylor couldn't show up for the interview. Most likely, cross her name off the list without a second thought as they had people lined up begging to work for them.

It was an opportunity she didn't want to miss, and it was up to Taylor to make it happen.

Chapter Seven

♥

HER MOTHER CAME INTO the kitchen, impeccably dressed and not a hair was out of place. Though the flare legged pants were out of style and must have been a recent addition to her wardrobe to cover the cast. It warmed Taylor's heart to see her mother pushing forward toward recovery and not finding her situation as one to stay in bed or by hiding out in her bedroom.

"Hey, Mom. Delores Sullivan, the woman in the Rabbit cabin, was asking about having her granddaughter, Trixie, come to visit for a few nights. Is that something you allow? I mean, I fully expected it to be fine, and hinted as much, but would like to stop by and confirm when I finish up the breakfast dishes."

"Good afternoon, dear. Of course, her granddaughter can visit. I love it when children are around, as the sound of their laughter always warms my heart. It's a small cabin but has a double bed. I'm sure they can bunk together. Just remember to add an extra person to the breakfast preparations while she's visiting. We also have a cot that can be set up in the cabin if she prefers." Her mother moved closer to inspect Taylor's handiwork for the charcuterie board filled with cheese, crackers, olives, and pickled beets, that she would put out for guests who wanted a snack before heading into town for dinner. Her mother seemed to blossom with the buzz of conversation as she mingled, playing host from the confines of her motorized wheelchair.

Taylor nodded. "Easy enough. The girl is five, so I don't expect she eats much."

Her mother nodded. "True enough. Oh, and would you be a dear and drop off an extra set of towels for them? I'll let your father know so he can be on the lookout for Delores to help with any luggage if you find out when they are expected to arrive."

"That sounds perfect." Her parents always made people feel special and welcome. Some things never changed, and Taylor was proud of the way they cared about everyone who visited. Their motto had always been...*a guest was family forever.*

"I just wish I could help more. This wheelchair is getting old. Which reminds me, I won't be able to take the little girl to the pumpkin patch." Her mother frowned, as though deep in thought, tapping her chin. "It's a tradition, you know. And the pumpkins are huge this year."

"Yes, I saw three or four of them on the front porch. You always have the nicest fall displays. The wheelchair won't be for long. You said two weeks, so you're almost halfway home." Taylor hugged her mother, hoping to encourage her.

"There's been a slight development that could change the timeline. My appointment with the doctor yesterday didn't go as well as I would have expected. He thinks I'm pushing it to be up and walking next week. I didn't want to say anything yet because I know you need to get back to California."

Not the best news. In fact, the worst. As much for her mother as for Taylor. "I do, but being here for you is more important. Most likely, it would be the end of my chances to get the job if I can't make the interview, but then, maybe it's not God's plan for my life if that happens." Taylor let out a deep breath. She had to keep her priorities straight, even though it was difficult now.

"Well, I'm sure we'll manage, dear. I'm grateful you came when you did, but if you get the call, you need to be there. But perhaps they will take longer than you suspect."

"Thanks, Mom. Let's just pray you're right. I love being home and helping. I've felt so unsettled lately, and I'm hoping the new job will fix that. Oddly enough, I've felt a sense of peace just being here with you and dad. Perhaps a trip home was just what I needed." Taylor would include more trips home, and not just when her parents needed her...but because she wanted to be home. With them.

Her mother patted her hand. "Like I said, we'll figure something out. I think I'll ask your father to run the child out to the pumpkin patch on the tractor. It's such a treat for the children. A highlight of visiting."

"That won't work. Don't you remember? Dad said he's headed into town to pick up some parts to fix the automatic gate controller. Sounds like it started acting up this morning. Maybe he can take her tomorrow."

"Oh, that's right. Good thing I have you around to remind me. Except tomorrow, your father has a full schedule with my doctor appointments. They're doing some follow-up MRIs to recheck the healing and make sure they didn't miss anything. *Hmmm*, there's got to be a way to get the child to the pumpkin patch." Her mother tapped her chin repeatedly, deep in thought. The instant her mother's gaze landed on Taylor; a smile lit her face. "I know. You could take her."

Taylor shook her head. "I haven't driven the tractor in years. Besides, having her in my lap wouldn't be all that safe. I'm sure Dad could squeeze in the time somehow."

"No, no, dear. You hook up the wagon, and it's already loaded with hay. *Hmmm*, unless the storm blew it out. Anyway, ask Randy to help you. I feel sure he would lend a hand for such a worthy cause."

Taylor had fallen right into her mother's trap. "Mom...we've been over this."

"What? It's just asking him to check the hay and hitch the wagon. Nothing interfering about that, is there?"

Her mother was right. It's not like she and Randy couldn't be in the same room or be friends. Yesterday they even talked and now she was helping him with the cleanup part of the repairs. How bad could it be? It's not like he would spend the afternoon on a sunny day wagon ride with her, which sounded far too romantic for her liking. "Fine. I'll talk to him."

"You will?" Her mother's radiant smile reached her eyes. It was as though years of tension lines melted away.

Taylor suspected this was her mother's plan right from the beginning. Let her mother have her fun...it's not like it would change the outcome. "Yes. I'm going to lend Randy a hand in the clean-up process this afternoon, so I'll ask him then."

"I didn't know you were helping with the repairs. That's so nice of you, dear." Too late, Taylor realized she'd just fed her mother fuel for the matchmaking plan.

"I'm simply trying to move things along, so don't go getting any ideas. Nothing has changed from our last discussion."

"Ideas about what?" her mother asked, feigning ignorance.

Taylor rolled her eyes. "You know perfectly well what I'm talking about. Randy and I are not getting back together. We are two different people on different paths in life, something you need to accept once and for all."

"I know, dear. I know."

"See that you remember it." Taylor gave her the stink eye as she walked out...putting her mother on notice to stay out of her personal business.

Chapter Eight

♥

Sporting a pair of fitted jeans and a T-shirt with the slo-gan *Jesus is my Co-Pilot*, Taylor was ready to start work. The shirt always made people smile, including herself. In her world, she considered it a staple part of her dress code to be worn under her charter pilot's uniform, which is why she had ten of them.

She loved the message, but lived and breathed it while flying high in the clouds. It was where she felt closest to God, and it was a reminder to trust Him in all things. Taylor slid on a pair of comfortable sneakers and headed for the great room. After pushing the plastic that hung over the opening, she stepped inside. Randy and Dane were engrossed in what they were doing, the buzz of the saw and spray of sawdust were proof they were hard at work.

There was still so much to be done, but at least it was coming together. The hole in the roof had been fixed and the drywall almost all hung and mudded, ready for a couple of coats of paint. Painting was something she wouldn't mind doing, and Taylor planned to plant the seed in Randy's ear.

Unsure of where to begin, she started toward him. His gaze drifted up to her as she approached, the silence of the machine quick to follow.

"Hey, there. I wasn't sure you'd be back to help today," he said, shooting her a wink as he stepped out from behind the table saw.

"Ulterior motives are handy motivators. So, what would you like me to do?"

Randy pointed to an enormous pile of debris that hadn't been there yesterday. "I pulled the damaged sheetrock down and busted it up to make it easy for you to haul outside to the dumpster."

Her focus had been on the rehung drywall and the need for paint, not the mess it made. A mess he wanted her to clean up. "I'm betting my parents loved the noise. Glad I was in my cabin."

Randy chuckled. "For your information, I was done by eight last night, and I wasn't that noisy."

"Right. Nothing about construction spells quiet." Taylor had gotten used to the early morning wake-up call of the jackhammer, but it didn't mean she liked it.

"I'm serious. I mostly used my hands and feet, leveraging the pieces first, and then doing a karate kick." Randy laughed, doing a side kick by showing her.

"As opposed to hammering at seven AM and waking everyone up?" she teased, reminding him of that daily transgression.

"The guests are up and about, and I checked with the guests first to make sure they were cool with me working that early."

Taylor frowned. "Seems you could have told me that before."

"And ruin all the fun? Not a chance." He laughed.

Taylor rolled her eyes. "Thank you." *Not.* "Nice pile. It should make it easier for me to haul out. So, thanks." If he stopped the noisy work at eight, chances are he was here even later to push everything into the pile...for her. Contrary to what Randy said, he had been expecting her to show up. The thought pleased her.

"You're welcome. See, it's easy to say the words," Randy teased.

So much for the moment of peace between them. "When deserved. I do, however, have a chance for you to apologize properly." It was the perfect lead in asking for a favor.

Randy frowned. "How's that? I didn't know an apology was in order."

It was Taylor's turn to smile sweetly. "Let's just call it helping each other."

"What do you want, Taylor?"

"There's a little girl arriving around four. She's Delores Sullivan's granddaughter, who is coming to stay with her for a few days. My dad is in town, and I was hoping you would get her luggage to the Rabbit cabin."

"Consider it done. It seems easy enough for a pardon for my wake-up call offense." Randy chuckled.

It was the second part of her request that was more difficult to ask. "Great."

"Nice shirt. Must be like heaven up there flying around," Randy said, his comment echoing her earlier thoughts.

Taylor nodded. "It is. And thanks. I own a dozen of these shirts. It's the motto I live by every time I fly the friendly skies."

"I like it. It suits you. Maybe someday you'll take me up for a ride. Before you leave town." The request caught her off guard.

She didn't take friends on joy rides. Well, all except Sandy. "Maybe. But only if you stop waking me up when it's still dark outside. There ought to be a law against that when I'm on vacation."

"Fine. No more hammering until after seven-thirty. See, I can be accommodating for the right reasons."

"I'll have to remember that. Deal," she said, grinning. The two of them were bantering much the same way they had as kids. Some things it would seem, never changed.

Randy nodded and then walked away, headed for the door.

Taylor grabbed one of the larger pieces of drywall and stacked smaller pieces on top, using the big one like a table. After carrying them outside to the dumpster, she retraced her steps and started the process all over. The work was simple, but exhausting. And dirty.

Randy had been gone for almost half an hour, and she wondered what was keeping him busy. Dane worked tirelessly but said little. Small talk clearly wasn't his forte.

She stopped to wipe the sweat off her brow, not caring that her hands were covered in chalky dust. Anything to keep the sweat from stinging her eyes. Taylor squinted when a couple of dust specks landed in the corner of one eye. Wiping at them only made the situation worse, as well as blur her vision. She took a step back to regroup, howling out loud as a stinging pain ricocheted through the bottom of her foot, causing her to pull back. A quick inspection revealed a nail embedded in the sole of her shoe. Luckily, it hadn't pierced through her skin, just enough pressure to make it hurt.

"You okay?" Dane called out.

"Just a nail...and it hurt like the dickens but didn't pierce the skin. I'll be fine. Thanks."

Dane nodded and went back to work.

Moving toward the wall, Taylor used one hand to brace herself as she placed the injured foot across her knee. It was a balancing act as she tried to pull the nail from her sneaker, and she was on the losing end of the battle to remove it. Work boots would have been a better idea, but most definitely a 20/20 after-the-fact idea at this point. Taylor gave the nail another sharp jerk and was relieved when it came free. But the wood stud she was using as a prop suddenly gave way under the pressure. Taylor kept herself upright and looked up at the ceiling to see if it might have caused any issues. The upper wall support board was at an odd angle without the stud in place. A few pieces of ceiling tile fell on her. Taylor looked up and frowned. Something was wrong. She took a step back, still peering at the ceiling to figure out the problem.

"Look out," Randy called, just as he caught her in his arms and thrust her out of the way. The ceiling brace tumbled down, some of the ceiling drywall with it, missing her by mere inches.

The reality of the situation stunned Taylor, shock keeping her from formulating any coherent words as she tried to piece together what just happened.

"Are you okay?" he asked, checking her over from head to toe.

Taylor nodded. "Y... yes. That could have crushed me." The reality of how close she'd come to being hurt stunned her. Randy's step-by-step process must have missed a step. One that could have proved costly. *To her.*

Randy pulled her closer, trying to comfort her. "But it didn't."

"Because of you," Taylor whispered, grateful he'd been nearby.

"Good timing. Maybe Jesus is your co-pilot down here on earth as well," Randy said, smiling as though trying to reassure her and portray an air of positive confidence.

Taylor found the comment soothing and knew he was right. "Thank you."

"What happened?" Randy asked, his gaze dropping to the new pile of debris that littered the floor.

She tried to remember the sequence of events. "I was using the stud on the wall as a support to get a nail out of my shoe and suddenly it gave way. I didn't think it was a big deal until pieces of the ceiling drywall started falling on me."

Lines of tension deepened across his forehead. "I just don't understand what happened. I always check the site every night. And I'm the one who pulled the sheetrock off this wall last night, and there wasn't anything loose." Randy scratched his head, a puzzled expression on his face. The lines of tension deepened across his forehead.

Accidents happen. "Maybe you missed it. It's not a huge deal because no one was hurt. It's a bigger mess and a lot more work. That's about it." It was her turn to make him feel better. This kind of thing would not sit well with Randy. Mr. Responsible all the way.

"You could have been hurt and I would have never forgiven myself. Honestly, you probably shouldn't work here anymore. Job sites are dangerous."

This she hadn't expected, and truth be told, she liked hard work. Flying didn't give her the exercise she needed, which explained all the sore muscles she had lately. "I'm not a frail flower."

"I'm also not looking to have trouble with the labor board or having my workman's compensation rates triple." Defensive language for a guy who had gone into protection mode. She knew Randy too well, not to see the signs.

"I'm not your employee, don't forget that. This is voluntarily helping you to help me." It was then Taylor realized Randy hadn't let her go yet. Feeling safe in his arms, she didn't want to move. But now, each second that passed made it more awkward. Emotions rushed through her she hadn't felt in forever. *Since Randy*. Perhaps it was just a bad case of adrenaline.

Randy shook his head. "No more, Taylor. I shouldn't have said yes."

This was an argument she wouldn't win. "Fine. I need one more favor, though. I'm going to take Trixie, the granddaughter of one of our guests, out to the pumpkin patch after they get here. If there is any way you would consider helping me hitch up the wagon? I would truly appreciate it. Mom wants me to drive her out there and I couldn't say no."

"No problem, especially as it gets you out of here." Randy shot her a wink to take the sting of his words, more reasonable now that she'd agreed. "Do you want me to go with you? It might be a lot to drive the tractor and watch the kid," he offered.

"Absolutely not. You need to stay here and work. Remember? Unless you've reconsidered and will let me help." She knew the answer, but it didn't hurt to ask.

"Not a chance. I'll meet you at the barn in an hour."

Taylor watched as he walked away, willing her emotions to take flight as well. Instead, the ache around her heart swelled to epic proportions.

Chapter Nine

♥

THIRTY MINUTES LATER, TAYLOR headed for Rabbit cabin to pick up Trixie for the pumpkin patch outing. Right on time, Delores Sullivan came outside, a young child holding her hand. Fair skin, blue eyes, and blonde bouncy curls that reminded her of Shirley Temple.

"Trixie, this is Miss Taylor. Mrs. Thompson's daughter...you know, the lady you just met who owns this lovely inn."

A frown marred the cherub's face. "The lady in the wheelchair?" she asked.

"Yes. That's her." Delores smiled at the child fondly.

"She was nice. Are you nice too?" Trixie asked.

"I like to think I am." Taylor grinned. "Do you want to go to the pumpkin patch with me and pick out your very own pumpkin?"

Trixie's eyes lit up. "I do. Grandma said I can pick any one I want. And I want one as big as the moon." She held up her arms and formed the biggest circle she could...which wasn't all that big, but Taylor understood what it meant.

Taylor grinned. "We'll have to search the whole pumpkin patch for the biggest one. My mother tells me they are huge this year, so I'm sure we can find something enormous, even if it's not as big as the moon." She held out her hand. "Ready to go?"

Trixie looked up at her grandmother. "Aren't you coming, Grandma?"

Delores shook her head. "No, sweetie. You run along with Miss Taylor. I'm too old for such gallivanting around the countryside on a wagon."

The little girl didn't seem entirely convinced.

Being in a strange place without a familiar face would be daunting, especially to a child. "I'll be with you the whole time and we will have so much fun. I can't tell you all the memories I have of doing the same thing with my father every year when I was a little girl. I grew up here and know every inch of the place."

Trixie looked back and forth between her grandmother and Taylor, then smiled. "Well, okay then. I really do want a pumpkin."

Delores hugged her granddaughter. "Then it's settled. Run along you two and let me get a quick nap," the older woman said.

Trixie moved closer and slipped her tiny hand into Taylor's. The universal sign of trust. "We are meeting a friend of mine at the barn, so let's go this way," she said, pointing to the left of the cabin.

"Is he coming with us?" Trixie asked.

Taylor waved farewell to Delores as they walked away. "No. He's got work to do here at the inn, but he's going to help us hitch up the wagon."

"I'm going on a wagon ride. Cool. I've never ridden in a wagon. This will be so much fun."

"It's the best. Bumping along the path through the meadows and the woods. Fun stuff." Taylor smiled, the memories flooding her all at once. She hadn't gone to the pumpkin patch in years. Not since she left home at eighteen, to be exact. This would be fun for her as well.

They approached the barn and discovered Randy had not only beat them there but had the wagon hitched. "This is a pleasant surprise. Thank you."

"No problem. Doing what I can to make it easy for you," he said.

The same as he had done years ago when they dated. It made her feel cherished, but perhaps this time around she appreciated it more. "Randy, I'd like you to meet Trixie."

"I know Mr. Randy. He helped me with my suitcase. Is he your friend?"

"Yes. And it sounds like we are ready to go, thanks to him."

"Yay! I'm getting a pumpkin as big as the moon," Trixie said, using her arms to form a giant, kid-sized circle for Randy's benefit this time.

"Wow. Let's hope Miss Taylor is strong enough to carry it," he teased, shooting Taylor a wink.

The man was incorrigible. "I'm strong enough...don't you worry, sweetheart. A woman can do anything a man can do. But a man can't say the same thing." Take that, tough guy.

"I don't understand. What can't he do?" Trixie asked in all innocence.

Taylor laughed. "Be a mommy." She shot Randy a *ha ha...top that expression because he would understand she meant having a baby.* Which was nothing she would come right out and discuss with a five-year-old, but she couldn't resist taunting the smug expression off his face.

"She has a point," Randy said, surprising Taylor with a comeback.

Trixie looked at her and then back at Randy. "One day, I'm going to be a mommy and have a baby girl. I think I'll name her...Arabella."

"I love that name. Shall we go? I promised your grandmother we would be back in time for her to take you into town for dinner. Let's get you up on the wagon and comfortable. You'll love the ride to the pumpkin patch. Be on the lookout for wildlife. It would be totally cool if we spot some deer or a fox, or even an elk. I saw one last week, though we don't see them often."

Trixie frowned. "If he's not coming with us, who's riding with me in the wagon?"

"I've got to drive the tractor, so you get to be a big girl and ride alone," Taylor said, hoping the child would find it one big adventure.

Trixie shook her head. "But I don't want to ride alone. It's scary. I saw a cartoon once and a little boy bounced right out when they hit a bump. Can I ride with you on the tractor instead?"

"No sweetie, it's not safe. I'm sorry. But this is your chance to be a big girl, and I'll be right here in the front close by." Taylor looked to Randy for moral support.

His answering smile caught her off guard. "How about I drive the tractor, and Miss Taylor rides with you?" Exactly what she had been trying to avoid.

Trixie nodded, her smile firmly back in place. "Oh, yes. I like that idea very much. Please, Miss Taylor." There was no way she would deny the child, and Randy knew it.

In the past, Randy had always been good at getting his way. Apparently, some things didn't change. The question was, why did he want to go? He had been just as much in agreement that nothing would be gained by opening the wounds to the past. And this certainly did just that, considering they had gone on many a wagon ride together. "Fine. Sounds like a plan. We better go." The sooner they got started, the sooner it would be over. Then perhaps her racing heart would slow down.

Randy picked Trixie up, settling her in the wagon on a bale of hay. He even covered the child with the blanket Taylor had tossed in for added warmth and comfort.

"Thank you, Mr. Randy. Come on, Miss Taylor, I'm ready to go," Trixie said.

Randy offered her his hand, but after a moment's hesitation, Taylor used the side rail and pulled herself into the wagon. It was a sweet gesture, but it would only confuse her heart more.

The dirt road to the pumpkin patch had lots of potholes, making the trip go longer than expected. Taylor pointed out a fox she spotted along the wooded edge. It would have been amazing to see the elk again, but so far, there'd been no such luck. Lots of birds flew overhead. She identified them the best she could, and Trixie tried her best to remember the names when they spotted them again. At five years old, Trixie asked a lot of questions, mostly wanting to understand the why of everything.

When they arrived, Randy shut off the tractor and hopped down, making his way to the back of the wagon to help them get off safely. "Was that a fun ride?" he asked, his gaze on Trixie.

"It sure was. I saw a fox, and an eagle, and a...what's that other gigantic bird? The black one?"

"A turkey vulture," Taylor said, knowing which one she meant.

Trixie nodded. "Yup. I saw a turkey vulture. But he doesn't look like the big turkeys on TV."

Randy chuckled. "It's not really a turkey, just the bird's name. I don't know why they call the poor thing that, but I will certainly look it up for you. We can both learn something."

Trixie's eyes grew wide when she spotted the pumpkin patch. "That's a lot of pumpkins," she said, as they drew near.

Taylor smiled as she remembered feeling the same way about the pumpkin patch. It wasn't as big as the commercial places, but it was special. And just like her mother said, there were some amazing pumpkins to choose from this year. "It sure is. And you can pick anyone you want. Just stay in the rows and walk all around to discover the perfect one for you. And perhaps you could pick a second one for your grandmother."

"She would like that." Trixie smiled.

Taylor walked behind her, while Randy walked one path over, pointing at different pumpkins and discussing their merits. Who knew he was such a pumpkin aficionado?

"Do you like the colorful ones, or the plain orange ones?" Taylor asked.

Trixie seemed to consider the question seriously. "The plain ones. Just like Charlie Brown. He found the perfect pumpkin. The other ones are pretty, but not like a real pumpkin. Maybe grandma would want one of those."

"I think that's a grand idea." They continued to check out every pumpkin, stopping to discuss each one that warranted a second look.

"Look at this, Trixie," Randy shouted, pointing down at the huge orange ball blocking his path.

"Wow. That's really big," Trixie said, her voice rising with excitement.

Randy stepped gingerly in the middle of the row, careful not to step on any of the vines as he crossed to their row. He reached for Trixie and lifted her in his arms, and then crossed back to the other path, setting her down close to the pumpkin.

"Thank you. I love it," Trixie said, her eyes shining. She kneeled and tried to wrap her arms around the pumpkin. "I can't get my arms around it, so I know it's really big."

"Then it's perfect for you," Taylor said. "Almost as big as the moon."

"Yup." Trixie beamed.

"Then it's settled. How about I carry this one back to the wagon and the two of you find one for your grand-mother? And Taylor, take a couple of them back to your mother. You know she loves coming out here and can't this year. The ones on the front porch are nice, but she likes some of the more unique ones and can decorate inside with them."

"Good idea. How do you remember that?"

"I remember a lot of things."

His comment left her to wonder what it meant, but somehow, she was inclined to believe he meant with her. It was getting harder and harder to remember why she didn't want him to tag along, or even why they broke up.

Ten minutes later, they had picked out their pumpkins and waited for Randy to return with the jackknife to cut them off the vine. Some folks like stem off, and some stem on, she was the latter. To her way of thinking, a stem added character.

Randy was on the phone, pacing back and forth. She waved in his direction to let him know they were ready to go and on a time schedule.

Trixie wandered through the patch, making sure she saw each pumpkin, in case she wanted to change her mind. They needed to get Trixie back to the inn, so Taylor was relieved when Randy headed their way.

"Everything okay?" she asked.

"Yes. Dane was asking about the new wiring we were installing in that one long wall. Your dad wants to run a few extra outlets and your mom wants a dimmer switch for better ambience. It's no big deal, but even minor changes will slow down progress. I'll have to run into town to pick up some extra parts later."

Taylor nodded, not surprised in the least. Randy wasn't one to get worked up over changes, preferring to find solutions. "I see. Well, hopefully, you can make up for today's outing. I hate to be the one who causes a delay."

"It will be done when it's done right. That's my motto. Though somehow, I need to incorporate driver and flunkey into my repair guy resume. Must be nice having me around," he teased.

"It is," she said. The honest answer slipped out before she could stop it. "But don't blame me, you offered."

"True. But then there wasn't much choice, was there? It was that or disappoint Trixie."

It was great he came along for the child, but what about her? Or perhaps she was reading too much into his attention. "You always were a softie at heart."

"For you," he quipped, reaching out to touch her face softly, like a caress.

Taylor's heart did a couple of somersaults, although everything else around slowed into non-existence.

"Can I switch pumpkins?" Trixie asked, coming to stand next to them, breaking into the moment.

Taylor was grateful for the interruption, but at a loss for words.

"Sure thing. Just lead the way," Randy said, following the little girl to her new discovery, and leaving Taylor staring after them.

It wasn't long before they were headed back to the inn. Trixie fell asleep in her arms, the little girl worn out from the adventure. Fresh air and sunshine had a way of doing that to a person. A nap wouldn't hurt before dinner, and she had a feeling Delores would be more than a little grateful not to have to deal with a fussy child.

But it wasn't the fresh air and sunshine influencing Taylor...it was Randy. Her heart was stirring to life, but the question was, how did she feel about it? She was leaving soon, and nothing good could come from resurrecting the past.

Chapter Ten

♥

"HAVE A GREAT DAY, Mr. and Mrs. Blackmore. Hope you have fun at your painting classes," Taylor said, collecting the dirty dishes from their breakfast table.

"Thank you, dear. Charles wasn't all that keen on doing art classes before, but he's more into it now since he came with me. Thinks he's the next Picasso," she teased, playfully slapping the older man's arm.

"Perhaps your own personal Picasso." Taylor grinned, joining in the fun.

Patty shook her head. "Ain't that the truth? After forty-seven years, I'm still in love with the big galoot."

Charles pulled his wife close. "Good thing, too...cause I'm not letting this woman go. Marriage is forever in my books."

Patty beamed under his attention. "You always say the nicest things. Glad I had the good sense to marry you the third time you asked."

"What can I say? It's either my irresistible nature or that I learned things along the way after being married for so long. Reckon you have me trained." Charles chuckled.

It was refreshing to see their banter, reminding Taylor of her parents. Once upon a time, they were like this. When did it end? Was the business too much for them? Or was it simply her mother's accident that temporarily stalled them out?

"Stop," Patty admonished. "Taylor will believe your nonsense."

Taylor laughed, shaking her head at their silliness. "Run along, you two. I want to make sure you come back here to celebrate your forty-eighth anniversary."

They disappeared, and Taylor took the dishes to the kitchen. She grabbed a basket to gather the rest of the table condiments in the makeshift dining room and the tablecloths.

The door opened and Taylor looked up, wondering what the couple had forgotten. Except it wasn't them. Instead, Jack stood there, his pearly whites flashing at her.

"Hey there. What brings you this way?" Taylor asked. They hadn't talked since their last outing, something she preferred.

"You," Jack said, straightforward and to the point.

"I see." She didn't, but it wouldn't take long for the guy to let her in on his reasoning.

"Do you?" he asked, stepping closer.

Taylor kept the basket in front of her. Almost like a security blanket. Not that she needed one, but it would stave off unwanted contact if Jack still thought there might be something between them.

Taylor chose to ignore his question. He was nice enough, perhaps more attentive than she preferred, but then that was more of her own issue rather than his. Lots of women would eat up the attention. She simply wasn't one of them. For her, relationships took time. And with Jack, the thought of kissing him netted her zero emotion or connection. He was solidly in the maybe-a-friend category, though the verdict on that one was still out. In high school, he was immature, but people changed. Grew up. And she was all for giving him a second chance to prove he was a changed person; one she might count on as a friend, but that's where it ended.

But then why not give Randy a second chance? The thought came out of nowhere and she pushed it aside. "What are you up to today?" she asked, not wanting to go down the path her thoughts were taking her.

"I'm headed to the art auction in Brambleton later. Every year, the park has this event and local artists display their wares. I consider it good exposure for meeting clientele. Thought you might like to join me," Jack said, formulating the invitation as though it were a given that Taylor wouldn't refuse.

The problem was…it sounded like fun. Not the business end of things…the artists displays sounded way more awesome. And there would be lots of people around, providing a safety net of sorts. "I would love the opportunity to check out local artists while I'm in town. You'd be surprised how many unique pieces are created by artists who might not be well known. I like to think it's an opportunity to discover someone before they make it big. Or simply to find something that draws me in spiritually. Speaks to me in a way that makes me feel alive."

Jack laughed. "A painting doesn't speak, but I'm glad you want to tag along. It'll be fun. Maybe we can catch some lunch after."

Another reminder of how different they were. "Okay. But Jack…just as friends." A reminder to Taylor's many other reminders seemed important.

"Fine." His smile slipped, but just a tad. He might not like her message, but it was clearly received.

"I'll meet you in town at the entrance to the park around eleven if that works for you?" Taylor suggested.

"Sounds good." Jack leaned forward and kissed her cheek before she could stop him.

"Sorry to interrupt," Randy said, his voice crisp with distaste.

Taylor jumped back. Though why, she didn't understand. It's not like she had anything to feel guilty about. "No, you're not interrupting anything. What's up?" she asked, not believing for a second that he was sorry.

"Your father needs some fresh towels delivered to the couple in the Bobcat cabin. He was on his way into town to get the oil changed in the truck."

"Okay, thanks. Sorry, Jack…I've got to run. See you at eleven at the entrance to the event. Isn't there a fountain there or something?"

Jack nodded. "Perfect. And yes, there's a fountain. I can't wait to have you all to myself." The satisfied smile he shot Randy was nothing short of infuriating.

"Be wary of a sheep in wolf's clothing, Taylor," Randy retorted.

It was like two children fighting in the sand box over a toy truck. *Childish.* And she wasn't a truck.

Taylor turned and left the room without so much as another word. Let the two of them duke it out. She wasn't interested in either one, so she didn't care what they did. Her own lie resounded firmly in her head. She cared about Randy, but there was nothing she could do about it.

Or wanted to do about it. Her life was in San Francisco.

She grabbed two fresh sets of towels and headed for the Bobcat cabin. Taylor inspected the room, and satisfied there wasn't anything else to be done in the way of picking up, she started out the door. Her phone vibrated, the ring tone alerting her to an incoming call. It wasn't a number she recognized, and she almost killed the call assuming it was spam.

Taylor pressed the answer button, in case it was the charter company. "Hello."

"Good morning. I'd like to speak with Taylor Thompson if she's available, please?" The man sounded quite formal, though still pleasant.

Was this the call she'd been waiting for? Highly unlikely as it was only seven AM on the west coast. Still, she couldn't stop the adrenaline rushing through her veins, her expectations high. "This is she."

"Bob Chandler from Alaskan Adventures. I've got your resume in front of me and I'm quite impressed with your experience. As you know, we narrowed down the list of qualified applicants to eight and were running background checks. You've moved to a list of eight candidates we would like to interview in person. I'll be conducting the interviews, and I'm setting the appointments. Is there any chance you could fly up here tomorrow or the following day? I apologize for the short notice, but my director really wants us to have things settled this week. We prefer to do an interview in person and then an in-flight test. This is an extremely challenging pilot's position, and we like to test out different scenarios. Like a real simulation."

Taylor paled. It was her worst nightmare come true. *A real simulation.* What if she choked? Not that it mattered. She couldn't leave North Carolina for at least another week. She tried to calm her rapid breathing and racing pulse. Perhaps it was God's writing on the wall. This wasn't the job for her. *Either that, or she was afraid, and it was an easy escape.*

Taylor didn't want to decide which was closer to the truth.

"Hello, Miss Thompson, are you still there?" Bob asked.

Taylor pulled herself together. "Sorry, I was trying to figure out a way to make the scheduled time work, but it won't. You see, I'm in North Carolina helping my parents with their B&B after they had some heavy storm damage. I couldn't possibly be there for at least another week." She let out a deep breath, feeling better after saying the words that would put an end to her chances with the company.

"Oh, I see. That is highly unfortunate. We had really hoped to finish all the interviews this week. I'm sorry if it won't work out. I can reach out to my director, though I'm not sure there's anything we can do to keep this open. In the meantime, please let me know if anything changes and I'll try to work you into the schedule."

"Thanks, Mr. Chandler. I appreciate your understanding." Taylor ended the call, deeply disappointed, but relieved. It was an odd mix of emotions for a position she really wanted. The thought of failing again was more than she could bare...but then so was *not* proving she could handle any situation thrown her way. *Like her father.*

All pilots were faced with the same challenges, but some jobs had a higher percentage of opportunity for something to go wrong. And then even that wasn't a guarantee. Every day a pilot took to the air...people's lives were in their hands. It was a daunting responsibility. And it was the same reason every six months she took updated simulator tests, just to keep her fresh and familiar with emergency protocol. She'd never failed another test...but it only took the one to have a devastating ending.

Perhaps in the end, this was God's way of showing her that she should continue to run regular charters.

Her safety net.

Chapter Eleven

♥

"I'M HEADED INTO TOWN, Mom. Do you need me to get any-thing?" Taylor asked her mother when she came into the living room.

Her mother's gaze sharpened, fixated on Taylor. "No thanks, dear. Something special going on?"

More than likely, her mother was hoping she and Randy would do something fun for a change. "There's an art show over in Brambleton that sounds like fun. I thought I would check it out for a bit before I needed to work on appetizers for tonight and breakfast." Giving all the facts served no purpose.

"Are you going by yourself? I could go if you don't mind all the extra work required to get me in and out of the car." Her mother was a smooth operator, forcing Taylor to reveal the whole truth.

"Actually, I'm going to meet Jack," she said, schooling her voice to a flat...and final tone. This wasn't up for debate. Her life was her own.

Her mother shook her head and frowned. "Don't tell me you're falling for his fake charm."

"Mother...stop. I keep telling you, he's not the same kid he was in high school. And I'm not falling for anyone. We're just friends and the art show sounded like fun." Taylor would love to pick up a local artist's work, something with loads of color to spruce up her bare bones' apartment.

Her mother huffed. "Well, make sure it's just friendship. I find him to be arrogant and conceited. A not-so-winning combination, no matter how good looking or how many teeth he shows when he smiles."

"Enough, Mom," Taylor was quickly reaching her threshold for trying the civil route. Knowing God would want her to hold steady and not be offended, she took a deep breath and exhaled.

"Well...it's true. Now take Randy, for instance. He's a nice guy. Maybe you should think about giving him another chance. I don't understand why you broke it off. Always thought the two of you would get married." The gloves were off, her mother's matchmaking exposed. And delivered without so much as a blink of an eye.

It irritated Taylor beyond belief, but not so much as it had when she first arrived. It was nice seeing Randy again, but that's where it stopped. "There's a lot you don't know. He's not the great guy you all seem to think he is."

"Why ever would you say that dear?"

Taylor was tired of looking like the bad guy in the breakup. "He was dating someone else...I mean, he started dating weeks after the breakup."

"I'm sure you're wrong. Randy loved you so much...and I'm not sure anything has changed."

"It wasn't hearsay. More like an eyewitness. I went to his college to talk about getting back together, but I was too late. His emotional attachment was short-lived, proof we weren't meant to be together."

"I'm so sorry, dear." Finally, an ounce of compassion from her mother. Sometimes, it would seem, the whole truth was better instead of bearing the pain alone.

"This is why it's awkward that you hired him with matchmaking plans. We don't belong together, and you need to accept that," Taylor pressed, wanting her mother to admit it out loud.

Her mother's guilty expression was all she needed for confirmation. "Can't blame a mother for dreaming. Did you ever ask him about it? There's always two sides to every story, and you need both to make such an important decision."

Hands on hips, Taylor shook her head. "Watching him hug and kiss a woman is more than enough proof. I didn't need to ask. You're meddling where you don't belong. I'm going back to San Francisco soon. Instead of concentrating on my love life, perhaps you should focus on the exercises the doctor gave you so that you can get back on your feet and get around easier."

"I'm doing them. Trust me, I'm all for getting out of this wheelchair, too. Your father's driving me nuts worrying over me."

Taylor smiled. "It's nice he cares. Maybe you should enjoy it instead of fussing. Later," she said, waving as she headed out the front door. Her parents had been married thirty-five years, and they were still in love. It was something Taylor wanted for herself. And once upon a time, thought she would have with Randy. For Taylor…life didn't seem to hold the relationship and family card.

She drove the truck the short distance to Brambleton and parked in the closest spot she could find to the park. Tents filled the grassy area, all lined up in rows for onlookers to peruse the various artists and their work. Making her way to the fountain by the entrance, she sat down to wait, since she was ten minutes early. Gazing at the sea of people visiting, Taylor was sure the event would be a success.

She spotted Jack talking with a woman, the two laughing at something he said. Jack dropped a kiss on the woman's cheek and walked away, heading straight Taylor's way. She couldn't help but notice the longing on the woman's face as she watched his departure. The woman was smitten, but then, with Jack, he oozed charm and probably attracted women like bees to honey. Which was another reason they would never suit. She wanted a one-woman man.

Jack smiled and reached for her hand, pressing it to his lips. It was an *ewww* moment, his hand warm and clammy. "I'm glad you could make it, Taylor."

She forced a smile to her lips and withdrew her hand from his. "Me too. This looks like fun. Thanks for asking." Perhaps in her quest for a fun outing, she should have reconsidered who she shared it with. The kiss worried her he might not have really accepted her refusal to see them as anything more than friends.

"You look beautiful, and I love the red dress," Jack said, shooting her a wink.

"This old thing?" Taylor laughed and shook her head. "It's the closest thing I could find that shouted artsy."

"You could wear anything, and you would look stunning. Shall we look around?" he said, once again taking her hand.

"Sounds good. I saw you with a woman before you met me. Is she your girlfriend?" Taylor asked, pulling her hand away. Again. Perhaps calling out his ladies-man personality would help send the message.

Jack frowned. "Hardly. Business client."

"Do you kiss all your clients?"

"Most…if they are of the female variety. Clients eat the attention up," Jack said, grinning like he held the world in the palm of his clammy hand.

Arrogant. Her mother's comment was more than a little spot on. "Or are misled…"

"*Hmmm.* Are you a little jealous perhaps? That would make my day," he said, grabbing her arm to stop her.

Taylor shook her head and let out a deep breath. "Nope. We are not at all suited, something I've already told you."

"Wow. Talk about crushing a man's dreams. But you can't blame me for trying."

"You're dreaming of a penthouse suite, not a wife," Taylor retorted, not one to fall for his sweet-talking words.

"Perhaps...but if it was you...the outcome might be different."

Taylor really needed to put an end to his attempts to make them into something they would never be. He was persistent, but way off base. "Shut up and get walking. Your compliments are getting so deep I may need wading boots soon." She shot him a smile to take the sting out of her words, but then turned and headed for the first row of tents, not giving him a chance to answer.

They walked, stopping briefly to look over the artwork. Taylor was grateful he had let the subject drop. Toward the end of the row, Taylor stopped, intrigued by the artist's work. An older man was talking to a customer, and Taylor took the time to appreciate the pieces on display. She loved the simple lines and colors used on the landscape, especially the billowing cirrostratus and altocumulus clouds, which looked real. Something she was an expert judge of considering she flew in clouds like this all the time.

"This is beautiful. Look at the way he makes the clouds and trees come alive," she said, holding the painting up for Jack to see.

Jack shrugged. "It's okay. I mean, it's nothing original. There are trees and woods everywhere you look unless you live in the city."

"Agree to disagree. The painting draws you in as though you are there. That's not always easy for an artist to accomplish." The artist's paintings spoke of a love and passion for the beauty of nature and seeing beyond the surface. The clouds came alive, serving as an inspiration for Taylor to get back up in the skies. It had been over a week since she flew here. Normally, she flew every day.

"If you say so. Ready to keep moving?"

Taylor shook her head. "I'm going to stay and talk to the artist a moment. You go ahead, and I'll catch up." His attitude was boring. It was as though he couldn't see anything beyond green tinted glasses. Money green. And Taylor didn't want him to rain on her excitement for this painting.

"Okay. I saw someone I wouldn't mind talking to about a business deal, so thanks."

"Just remember, some people are here for fun and to relax," she chided. All work and no play...made Jack a dull boy. The old saying couldn't have been more spot on.

"Yes, but people like me are here to scout out new clients. Never miss an opportunity, is my motto."

Taylor shook her head but said nothing as he walked away. People like Jack never really understood or appreciated all the surrounding beauty, so caught up in business they missed out on life. A tap on her shoulder had

Taylor spinning around. "Sandy! What on earth are you doing here?" she wrapped her best friend in a bear hug before giving her a chance to answer.

"It's good to see you, too, bestie." Sandy grinned. "Your warm welcome makes the drive here worth every second."

"But why are you here? You didn't say a word about coming. Are you with someone?" Taylor glanced around to see if anyone had stepped forward.

"I didn't say anything because I wanted to surprise you. The boss let me take the day off, so I jumped at the opportunity to visit. There was no way I was letting you come to North Carolina without the two of us getting together. And no, there's no one with me." Sandy gazed down at the painting Taylor held. "That's gorgeous. Are you buying it?"

"I am." She glanced at the artist, only to find him still in his discussion. "How did you know where to find me?"

"Your mother. Sounds like I got to the inn not long after you left. She was all about making sure I found you. It was odd she was so adamant that I rush over here to find you. I was beginning to think she didn't want me hanging around," Sandy teased.

"Not odd, and quite the opposite. She's not happy I came to the event with Jack Tinsdale. My mother had an ulterior motive in making sure you crashed our outing." But for once, Taylor couldn't find it in her heart to be upset. Not only was it great to see her friend, but this was the excuse she needed to dump Jack.

Deep grooves rippled across Sandy's forehead. "*Umm*, no way. Please tell me you and Jack aren't an item."

"No...not me and Jack as a couple. Hardly. We're just friends. He seems okay now that he's more mature. Not the same jerk he was in high school."

"*Hmmmphh*. Hard to believe."

Taylor rolled her eyes. "You sound just like my mother."

"So where is this new Jack?"

"I sent him ahead so that I could talk to the artist and buy the painting. Jack is not much into art."

"And that's why he invited you to an art show?" Sandy teased.

Her friend made a good point. Jack was here for clients or to further their relationship. Nothing about this outing said friendly fun. "He's canvassing for clients. For him, it's business."

"So, if it's not you and Jack...what's going on with you and Randy? I saw him at the inn. Hard-working guy and handsome to boot. He seems to have gotten better with age. I'm sure you noticed."

Taylor *had* noticed, but it wasn't the point. "He always looks good, but nothing is going on there either. What we had is in the past and I'm going back to California."

"You were both young, and when feelings get hurt, there's no telling how someone will react." Sandy's point was valid, but it wasn't one Taylor wanted to accept or make allowances for when it came to her perspective on the past.

"Still…who moves on that fast? We were together for two years. I got scared and made a mistake breaking it off, but then he moves on as if the two years meant nothing." The image of him holding another woman at the college party was never far away. He held the woman tight, and it was no short embrace…and then they kissed. Taylor couldn't leave fast enough, not wanting Randy to see that she had come crawling back.

"So, fix the mistake. It's not too late. You're both still single. Ever wonder why?" Sandy was pressing her to think and feel about Randy in ways she hadn't for years.

It still hurt too much, though why, she should certainly give some thought to. Not now though. Right now, she was excited to see Sandy. "It's too late. We lead different lives, so let it drop."

"If you say so. Just remember, I know how you felt about him. Still feel about him. Best friends can't hide the truth."

"Rubbish." *Or not*…Taylor wasn't entirely sure anymore.

"Name me one serious relationship you've had since you broke up with Randy eight years ago?" Sandy asked.

Taylor smiled. "Flying. Flying is my life."

"That's a career. Not someone you marry and start a family with. Not someone to grow old with."

"Enough. There's time for that later if it is meant to be. Only God knows the plan for my life. And once I know I'm good enough to be a pilot, maybe then I'll slow down and consider the options."

Sandy shook her head. "You are already good enough. That's why you have a pilot's license. You've got to let the past go."

"I can't. Not yet. But if I get this job in Alaska, the challenges will put me to the test. Then I'll know."

"That's what you said about the job you have now, and the job before that. You sound like a broken record." Sandy wasn't pulling any punches, but then that's what best friends were for.

"Perhaps it's the broken part that rings true. Let's go get some lunch and talk about good things. Catch me up on everything going on, including *your* boyfriends. There must be someone special you're interested in."

"Sounds good. But what about Jack?"

"Hang on. I'll call him and explain. I doubt he'll even notice I'm gone." Taylor called him but kept getting his voice mail, so she left a message. "Done. Just give me a few minutes to talk to the artist and buy this, and then we can skedaddle."

Taylor kept the conversation short, pleased with her purchase. She turned back to Sandy. "Let's go. So, what should we talk about first?"

"Dane Prince." Nothing could have shocked Taylor more than her friend's answer.

"Interesting. I'm guessing you met the guy who works for Randy. What do you want to know about him...and why?" Taylor pressed.

"Why? You shouldn't even have to ask. Yes, I met Mr. Dreamy and I want the scoop. That is one fine man, and his chocolate brown eyes won me over at hello." Sandy's flushed cheeks told more of the story. Her friend was smitten.

Taylor laughed. "He's single, nice enough, but somewhat reserved. Randy met him in college, but that's about all I know. You'll have to find out the rest on your own."

"Oh, trust me, I plan to. But can't say as I would use the word reserved to describe him. We talked quite a bit. After lunch, I think we should head back to the inn."

Either they weren't talking about the same man…or Dane was more than a little infatuated with Sandy as well. Taylor was happy for her friend…if it were the case. The years she had been in love with Randy were the best. "So much for coming to see me," Taylor teased.

Sandy pulled back, one hand to her heart. "Except I am here to see you. Dane is a nice bonus. And I was hoping you'd take me for an air spin," she said, exaggerated hurt lacing her voice.

"Good answer." The idea of taking her plane up for a flight held great appeal, and she was more than willing to forgive Sandy.

Chapter Twelve

♥

THE ALARM CLOCK BUZZED, signaling it was time for Taylor to force herself out of bed, knowing the spinach and ham quiche and croissants wouldn't make themselves. Sandy left late last night after they had watched a movie and Taylor hadn't been able to fall asleep until she got her friend's text that she'd made it home okay. The offset, of course, was seeing Sandy and taking her up in the plane. They'd flown over the area, an aerial view Taylor knew well. There had been no sign of the elk, but she wouldn't give up hope of spotting the enormous, yet beautiful animal.

Slipping into a comfortable pair of jeans and donning her favorite beige cable-knit sweater, she pulled on a jacket and her boots and hurried to the main house to avoid the bone-chilling cold. The house was still dark and quiet. Leaving her boots at the front door so as not to track mud, she started down the hall using the light of the moon to find her way, the lure of a strong cup of coffee calling her name. Halfway there, she stepped into something cold and wet. Her first thought would have been a pet mess, but they didn't have pets at the lodge.

Taylor shook her phone to turn on the flashlight and was shocked to see water everywhere. Something was seriously wrong, and she needed to get her father. Racing back down the hall, she flipped on the overhead light and then knocked on their bedroom door. "Dad, get up. There's a problem out here and I need you." She knocked again. "Dad, can you hear me?"

The bedroom door opened. "What's wrong, Taylor?"

"I don't know, but there's water everywhere in the hallway. I figure I better come get you so we can find out what's happening. I have no idea how bad it is yet." Taylor grabbed her boots and pulled them back on.

"Hang on, let me grab my boots, too. This isn't good. Wayward water has a historical way of wreaking havoc in a home, and I can't imagine what's going on. We don't need more problems, but it looks like we got them anyway." Her father grabbed his boots and sat down, making short work of pulling them on. "Let's go. You check the kitchen, and I'll check both bathrooms. Those are the only primary water sources on this side of the house. It can't be our bathroom because the water is not in our room."

Taylor headed for the kitchen, her father right behind her, sloshing through almost an inch of water. She reached the counter and pulled open the double cupboard doors to the sink to check the hoses. Her father disappeared behind the plastic drop cloth.

The bottom of the sink cabinet was dry, and the dishwasher hoses fed into the same area.

"Found the problem," her father called out from the other side of the plastic. There was a bathroom there for the guests in the great room area. Except that the room was under repair, which meant the bathroom wasn't in use.

Taylor crossed the kitchen, ducking under the plastic to join her father.

"What the devil is going on?" Randy asked, coming in from outside through the side door of the great room.

Taylor shook her head. "I don't know, but it sounds like my father found the problem. There was water everywhere when I came in a few minutes ago."

"This is a complication I didn't need." Randy ran a hand through his hair, his jaw firmly clenched. "Where is he?"

Taylor pointed to the bathroom in the corner. "He's back there."

"That makes even less sense. No one uses that bathroom, since it's not even functional at this point."

Exactly the same thing Taylor had rationalized out, but it didn't change the result. "Let's go see what the issue is." The two of them found her father mopping up the floor with the towels that had been hanging on the wall.

"What's going on?" Randy asked, grabbing more towels from the closet and laying them out on the floor. Not that it was doing much good. There was simply too much water. "Is there a leaky hose?"

Her father looked up and shook his head. "I wish it was that simple, given that none of this is ideal. The water faucet was left running, and it would seem some drywall had fallen in the sink and clogged the drain. Eventually, the pieces plugged even the overflow safety hole," he said, tension radiating from his words. Five AM and flooding waters would have that effect on anyone.

"That's impossible. We don't use this bathroom. We have a porta-potty set up out back." Randy had grown defensive, at a loss to explain what appeared to be worker error.

"Maybe Dane had to make an exception and forgot," Taylor offered, trying to think of likely reasons for the mistake.

"No, he wouldn't. But seeing as there's no way to determine who's at fault, I'll pay for the damages. I don't understand what's going on. First the wall collapses and now the drain is clogged, and the faucet left running. This doesn't look good, and I'm sorry, Mr. Thompson. I've never had these types of issues before and I promise nothing else will happen."

"I don't know...doesn't seem fair if it's not your fault," her father said, though Taylor could tell he would prefer to accept the generous offer.

"The sooner we get the water out of here, the less damage there will be. Dad, can you send the guests to the diner in town for breakfast this morning? Randy, Dane, and I will clean up the mess. Then we can assess the situation." Taylor was in take charge mode, knowing the decision of responsibility and expenses was best assessed after they put the problem to bed.

Her father nodded. "Sounds like a good plan. Let me tell your mother what's happening before she gets out of bed. I think her injuries have worn her out more than she cares to admit, and she's been quite tired. This will have her itching to get back to work and stressing over every detail."

Randy heaved a heavy sigh. "Thanks, Taylor. I'm sure you'd rather be cooking breakfast than helping save my butt. I still don't understand, but agree, there's a time and place to look into this matter further."

"Don't be too sure of that," she teased, trying to lighten the somber mood.

"I'll be back soon to help," her father said, handing her the already sopping wet towel.

"I'll get the mop and broom. We need to push the excess water out the door and then dry everything the best we can." It was a daunting task, but with everyone pitching in to help, they could have this under control in no time at all.

"At least we're not in danger of the water coming in contact with the electrical system. I just wish I could understand what happened," Randy said, the weight of the world on his shoulders.

Her father left the room.

"It was nice of you to offer to pay for the damages," she said, wanting him to know that she wasn't upset with him.

"Not nice. *Right.* Your folks have been good to me and if there's any chance either myself or an employee of mine is responsible, then I plan to do the right thing."

"You always did." *Except for once.* But then, what did it matter how short or long before Randy moved on from their relationship? She was the one who made the mistake of breaking it off. Technically, Randy had done nothing wrong. But it wasn't the technicality that bothered her...it was the emotional side of things. Because even now, her heart was over him.

Randy's gaze never wavered but he said nothing. If only she could read his mind, because it sure looked like he had a lot to say.

It took a better part of the day to finish cleaning up the mess. Luckily, the water hadn't sat long enough to do damage to the hardwoods. If it had been laminated flooring, the outcome would have been entirely different.

"Sorry, but I've got to head out a little early today," Dane said, coming to stand next to them.

Randy frowned. "We lost a whole day of work, and I was hoping we could put in a few more hours this evening to make up for it."

Dane shook his head. "No can do, boss. I've got a hot date."

"Anyone I know?" Taylor teased, already knowing full well who he was going on a date with. Dane and Sandy had taken a walk last night and her friend was all too willing to update her. The two planned to meet halfway, which was still quite a drive. *The heart wants what the heart wants,* Sandy had reasoned.

"Like you don't know," Dane said, grinning. "I mean, is she for real? Sandy, that is. She seems too good to be true, though I barely know her."

Taylor laughed. "I've known her for a long time and she's the real deal. But if I were you, tread slowly. She's been burned before and though she's quick to get interested, it's what happens afterwards that sends her running in the opposite direction. If you're looking for a little fun but over and done kind of relationship, she's not the girl for you." She would do anything to protect Sandy from someone who would hurt her. The two had agreed a long time ago to intervene if they felt necessary.

"Good, because I'm not that kind of a guy, the fun and done kind, that is. Thanks for sharing...and caring. It's nice she has such a good friend." Dane left, a cheerful smile plastered on his face, reminding her of a little boy at Christmas.

"I've got to run your mother to her doctor's appointment. Dr. Sheraton agreed to wait a little longer today after I explained what happened," her father said, retrieving a sweater from a kitchen chair and sliding it on.

"Okay. Let me know how it goes." Her father disappeared past the plastic, leaving her and Randy alone.

Chapter Thirteen

"GUESS IT'S JUST THE two of us. Care to sit down on the porch with a glass of iced tea? I somehow feel as though we deserve the rest."

"For once, I couldn't agree with you more," Randy said, letting out a deep breath.

Taylor gathered up the rest of the wet towels. "Let me just start another load of wash. Wouldn't want to run out of towels for the guests." She couldn't help but feel sorry for Randy. The guy was doing everything he could to complete the repairs as quickly as possible, but he seemed plagued by problems. And she believed him when he said this wasn't normal.

"It was so nice of everyone to agree to go to the diner this morning," he said when she returned to the room.

She poured two glasses of tea, and they headed for the porch. "Business is slow enough as it is, without losing what we have, according to my parents. Do you know what's going on with the inn? I hadn't realized my parents even had problems." Taylor found them two spots on the porch swing that sported full sunshine for the radiant warmth.

"I reckon it's the new B&B over in Davenport. They're offering casino junkets to Cherokee and train expeditions via the Great Smoky Mountain Railroad with special themed attractions."

"I see. My mom mentioned the railroad and the casino earlier. My folks won't join the casino band wagon and I concur. I suppose they could try to connect with the railroad and put together something similar...but then it's just a repeat offering." If only she had known sooner, perhaps things wouldn't have gotten this bad. Though what she could do about it from the west coast wasn't a straightforward answer.

"This B&B is also further from the airport, which makes it more difficult to access. And honestly, your parents have done nothing to update their website since it went live fifteen plus years ago, and it shows. Sorry to be the bearer of bad news, but the facts are all there. Your folks are in trouble if something doesn't change."

Taylor searched her brain for answers. Anything to help. "It's something I've been meaning to check out, but I just haven't had the time. I thought Sandy could help me since she understands web design better than I do. Maybe she can update it and draw more attention to the rustic experience offered here. She was a whiz with that kind of stuff in high school. The only problem is it sounds like she's super busy at the hospital." Sandy would do anything for her parents if Taylor asked, but was it fair to take up her time?

"I've got another idea. Maybe you and I could fix it. I set up my website, and I know you have one. Between the two of us, surely, we could bring them into the twenty-first century." Randy shot her a wink, the easy camaraderie between them a flash from the past.

It was a good idea, but there was only one problem. "First off, Sandy designed mine. And though it's sweet of you to offer, there's not enough time. I'll be leaving soon." Not to mention, fixing the site was one thing, figuring out what it needed was an entirely different matter.

"For the new job?" Randy asked, one eyebrow quirked up in surprise.

"Not by the sounds of things." Taylor let out a deep sigh. The idea she would miss out on the opportunity still rankled, but helping her folks was more important. Perhaps God was sending her a message the Alaskan Adventures job wasn't right for her. Maybe He knew she wasn't up to the task.

"What do you mean?"

Taylor shrugged. "I got a call yesterday. They wanted me to come in for an interview but I'm here until next week at least. I can't leave my parents high and dry when they need me most, so I reckon I'm out of the running. But I do still have a job to go home for and can't stay any longer than necessary."

Randy reached out and laid a hand on her shoulder. "I'm sorry. Truly. I know you had your heart set on the job."

"I did." She nodded, very much aware of the connection between them, yet not wanting to give credence to her racing heart.

"Why did you have your heart set on it? I mean, Alaska sounds exciting, but flying brings you joy. I would think it's the sky, not the location that holds all the winning cards." Randy always had a way of putting things into perspective, but then, there was something he didn't know about her. Something that still had the power to drive her decisions.

Not that she'd be sharing that tidbit of information now…or ever. Perhaps a variation would suffice. "Honestly, it was the challenge. To prove that I'm good enough. My dad was an amazing pilot and won medals of honor for his bravery and service. A part of me wants to know that *I'm* good enough. Like my father. Not that I want something bad to happen, more that I'm qualified to handle whatever is thrown my way." It was the truth, and Randy didn't need to know why. Especially given Taylor tied her failed simulation test to her breakup with him and his all-to-soon defection with another woman.

Randy finished his tea and stood facing her. "You have your pilot's license and your medical flight certifications. That tells me someone thinks you're good enough to handle emergencies. Why would you need anything more?"

Taylor clenched the glass she held. A piece of paper didn't tell you anything. Only the real world and a real emergency would ever reveal one's deepest fears and whether they could rise above them to take charge. Luckily, ninety percent of pilots never faced the reality of an in-air emergency. Forcing herself to relax her grip, she tried to think of a response. "That's what they say." There was no way she could explain without dredging up the past.

"In other words, you're not going to expand on your comment."

"Exactly." Taylor shot him a hint of a smile to ease the rebuke. "We aren't a couple anymore and doing the tell all doesn't apply."

"True. But since you brought up the subject of us being a couple first, there is something I want to ask you. And since we have a rare moment of privacy, this is the perfect opportunity." Randy leaned against the porch rail, arms crossed, and lines of tension deeply etched across his forehead.

Taylor frowned, not sure where he was going with the conversation, but more than a little concerned, given his serious demeanor. "I can't imagine what this is about, but shoot."

"I want to ask you about something that happened in the past. Our past."

"Oh, no. Let's not delve into something we can't change. It's why they call it the past, and we agreed not to go down memory lane." Bringing up old heartaches would only make her heart ache more...not less. Even more reason to avoid the subject at all costs.

"Except your mother seems to think I ran you off."

Taylor jerked back. "My mother? What's she got to do with us aside from mistakenly playing matchmaker while I'm visiting? Something I've already told you."

His steely gaze never left her face, causing her to squirm. "Your mother stopped me before I left last night, and we chatted for a bit. Or more like, she talked, and I listened."

"I know how those conversations go. But what exactly did she have to say that's warranted this conversation now?" Taylor should never have told her mother the truth. Mrs. Fix-It was butting in where she didn't belong, or so it seemed. Better to know how much her mother told him if she wanted to downplay the situation.

"She thinks I cheated on you," Randy said, running a hand through his hair as though to diffuse tension.

"I never said that—" Taylor said, covering her mouth to stop any other admission from slipping out. Her answer was more than enough for Randy to know she'd said something to her mom and that it wasn't all a tall tale pulled out of mother's Sunday bonnet.

"Then what did you tell her? Because we both know that's not true. You broke up with me and never looked back. I waited for you to change your mind, to get settled into school and see that things could work...but you never did."

He was right about the first part, but wrong about the second. On this score, it was time to set the record straight...between the two of them. It would finally give her a chance for closure on the hurt he'd inflicted all those years ago. "You didn't wait long."

Randy frowned. "What are you talking about? It was a year before I even went on another date. You didn't think

I would stay single the rest of my life, did you? Though the fact I'm still alone should tell you something." The admission rocked her.

His version wasn't at all how she remembered things. "It was more like weeks. You moved on with some pretty brunette. I know because I came home to tell you I was sorry, and that I was wrong to run from our relationship out of fear. Contrary to what you seem to believe," she ground out.

"You did?" Randy asked, taking a step closer.

She nodded. "I did." It was a moment she would never forget. A moment etched on her heart forever.

Randy let out a deep breath. "Wow. I had no idea. I wish I had though, as I feel like we have wasted a lot of time. You should have talked to me, Taylor. I deserved more than an email breakup and years of silence."

"We have wasted nothing. You moved on," she insisted, trying to maintain control of the conversation. She wasn't the one whose feelings had defected to someone else.

Randy shook his head, moving closer still. "But I didn't. That woman you're talking about was Eric Fielding's wife, and I was comforting her after my friend died suddenly. She didn't have an easy time with it."

Taylor suddenly felt like a fool. How could she have been so wrong about everything? Or was it that her fears refused to allow her to think of any other options? To give Randy a chance to explain. The phrase young and dumb came to mind. "Oh." What else could she say?

"Exactly." Randy took her hand and drew her up close.

His nearness unnerved her. "I'm sorry I misjudged you, but it was never going to work between us anyway. Maybe that's why I believed what I saw. It was easier to keep things the way they were, than to go back and have a second break-up months later." She was still trying to defend her actions, though the sad truth gripped her like a vise. She'd wronged Randy, the man she once loved...twice.

"Thank you. And for the record, I don't believe we would have broken up again." He pulled her into his embrace.

"That's where you're wrong. You came back to Moonridge, and I wanted to experience the world. Our hearts are in two different places," Taylor said, trying to justify her choices...right or wrong. It was far easier than believing she'd made a colossal mistake.

Randy put a finger under her chin and tipped her head up, forcing her to look at him. "Our hearts belong together. Maybe that's why we are both single. We've been given this chance to change the outcome. Won't you give us a second chance?" He lowered his head slowly, giving her time to decide.

Taylor shook her head and stepped back. As much as her heart might want the fairytale ending, she was old enough for her wants not to hurt her. Okay...so hurt, yes, destroy...no. She would survive, just like she always did. Having managed the past eight years on her own, she could do it again. "Except we are still in two different places in life."

"It doesn't have to be this way. You said you didn't think you would get the job. Why not come home and start your own charter business? It's a win all the way around. You're still flying, we can be together, and you can help your folks." His hand caressed her cheek.

"It's not that easy. I'd rather get the job in Alaska. And as to coming home, I've never been one to want parental scrutiny all the time. And you and I, there's no way to know if we could ever make it work."

"That's true. But we've always been good together. Should still be together and you know it. It gives me hope because you didn't outright reject the idea. And you wouldn't be living in the same house with your parents." Randy chuckled.

Taylor nodded. Randy was right on every score, but it didn't add up to what she envisioned for her future.

"Truth is, I have considered branching out on my own, but I'm not ready for that leap of faith." There was a sense of home that continually called her back to Moonridge, though all she ever wanted to do was leave. And now, the call still wasn't strong enough to override the bigger issue…her fear of failure and having everyone discover the truth about her past failure. Taylor stepped away, his nearness rattling her emotions and making it difficult to think straight.

"When will you be?" he asked, his voice low and warm like a caress.

It was on the tip of Taylor's tongue to tell him the truth, but she couldn't say the words. Losing his respect would be harder than losing him, because this way she still had her memories and it would seem, strangely enough…his love. He thought she was a top-notch pilot. Shattering that illusion would change everything.

"Maybe never. I don't know. I would be the one giving up everything to come back here…hardly seems fair. The Alaskan Adventures job was my first choice and if I get it, which doesn't look promising at this point, then I wouldn't have come back. Everything else…you and I, coming home, a new business…well those things would always be my second choice."

"I prefer to think about all that you would gain, but you're right. I wouldn't want to be your second choice.

In time, it would sour things, knowing you held regrets close to your heart and not me." Randy picked up their glasses, an aura of sadness around him as he headed for the door. It was as though he'd lost his best friend...for the second time.

Randy didn't understand.

The truth was...if she didn't get the job, coming home would include Randy and might be her first choice. She cared about him...might even still love him. But then, coming home would be a first choice at that point only because her other first choice failed. And although failure was a great catalyst for change, it was not something to base a relationship on.

Besides, what if their situations were reversed? Would Randy come to Alaska for her? Somehow, she doubted it because he never wanted to move away from Moonridge the first time around. This was his home. It was hers too, originally, just not now.

Though Alaska wasn't hers yet either and probably never would be unless she could find a way to get home sooner. Something she couldn't do to her parents.

Chapter Fourteen

♥

Taylor avoided going past the staging area for the construction to avoid running into Randy. Things were awkward enough as they were, without actively seeking more chances to run into him. With a few minutes to spare before she headed to the kitchen to plan tomorrow's menu, she rocked on the porch of her cabin, trying to rationalize the conversation with Randy. It had come as a shock to realize she'd been wrong about him. But no matter how much she went over the situation, nothing changed. They still lived in two different worlds.

The sound of a woman's laughter drifted on the light breeze, capturing Taylor's attention. Call it curiosity, she made her way across the yard toward the sound. She was surprised to see a woman standing closer than normal to Randy, one hand on his arm. The last time she witnessed him in action, Taylor misjudged the situation. A mistake she wouldn't make again.

Forgetting her vow to steer clear of Randy, she approached them. "Hello. I saw we had a new guest, so I thought I should come welcome you to our B&B." Taylor was positive the woman wasn't a guest, but it was the perfect excuse for her presence.

"Oh, I'm not staying here." The woman frowned, her crease lines more heavily accented due to the thick layer of foundation make-up. Her perfectly coiffured brown hair barely moved in the breeze. "I'm Patty Stallings, one of the town council members," she added, her voice aloof.

"Good. Then I didn't miss the memo on a new arrival." Taylor smiled. "What brings you our way? Do you need to speak to my mother and father?"

"That won't be necessary. I've already talked to your father, and I'm mostly here to see Randy." The woman's voice became sugary sweet, leaving no doubt in Taylor's mind she wanted to more than '*see*' him.

Taylor turned slightly to block the woman's view as she rolled her eyes at Randy. "I see."

He shook his head. "Probably not. I have it on good authority you like to jump to conclusions." His comment stung.

"Whatever. So exactly what business does she have with you then?" Taylor pressed, not willing to let Randy sidetrack her.

"The historical project I told you about."

Patty laid a hand on Randy's arm and stepped closer. "I just had to come see for myself what all the fuss in town was about."

"Fuss?" Taylor asked.

"Well, it seems there's been some costly mistakes made on the repairs here. The council asked me to verify first-hand the situation, so here I am." Taylor was willing to bet Patty volunteered for the right to come out here, judging by the way she clung to Randy and his every word. Though how all the details of the events happening here at the inn made their way into the community gossip chain, she didn't have a clue.

"I've explained to Patty the mistakes are not my norm and they've been handled," Randy offered.

"He has graciously showed me around, and I must agree with his assessment. Randy is on top of the situation. Besides, your father has already vouched for Randy's work and agrees the issues were minor and being blown out of proportion. And as a well-respected member of the community, your father's stamp of approval will go a long way in Randy's run for the project lead. Crazy things can happen on job sites, but it's the caliber of the construction company that determines the outcome. We want only the best for the historical projects. We've narrowed it down to two companies, and I'm all too happy to report to the town council there's no justifiable reason to rule out Renovations by Design." Her long-winded answer was spoken like a true politician. All that to say, Randy was still in the running, which was excellent news.

Randy was more than a little relieved, the corded muscles of his neck relaxing a fraction. "Thank you for the honor, Patty. This means a lot to me."

It was on the tip of Taylor's tongue to ask who the other company was but felt it might not be right to know before it was announced. Curiosity won out. "Who's the other company? Or am I not allowed to ask?" Taylor was almost positive Patty would love being in the know and the opportunity to share.

"It's no secret. Clayton's. Jack Tinsdale is the rep, and I'm sure you remember him. His company is much bigger and perhaps capable of handling more than one project at a time. Though bigger isn't always better. It won't be long, and the council will make their final decision. As much as I would love to stay and chat, I've got to run. You know, a councilwoman's job is never done. Would you like to go to dinner tonight, Randy? It would be a great opportunity to discuss the historical project further, and perhaps you could give me more insight into your vision for the future of Moonridge."

That's not all the woman wanted to discuss.

"Sounds good to me. I've got some amazing ideas I'd like to share," Randy said, his broad smile like the warm sunshine. *Except it was aimed at the wrong woman.*

"Great. Let's say seven at Luigi's. I'm in the mood for some good Italian food and wine," Patty said, stepping away, her smile nothing short of his.

A happily matched pair.

"Perfect. I'll see you then." Patty waved as she headed for her car.

Taylor frowned at Randy. "Nothing like playing yourself into a winning hand," she scoffed.

Randy shook his head. "It's good business. Sorry you don't approve, but it's not your call."

Taylor was seeing green. "Maybe we'll run into each other tonight," she said before she could reconsider the words.

"How's that?" Randy asked.

"Jack asked me to dinner. It would be funny if we ended up in the same place." He had asked, but she had turned him down.

Randy scowled. "Guess I should get back to work since the boss's daughter is watching."

"Good idea. You're already behind schedule." So much for the easy camaraderie they shared earlier. Of course, that vanished after she rejected his offer of them as a couple. Again.

When Randy talked to her out on the porch and she assured him there was no chance for the two of them, it hadn't meant she wanted to see him with someone else. The least he could do was wait until she returned to California. The idea of sitting at home like a wallflower while Randy was out on the town prompted her to say what she did. Hopefully, Jack hadn't already found another date.

She pulled out her phone to send him a text.

Taylor: Reconsidered. Still available for tonight?

Jack: Absolutely. Pick you up at seven.

Taylor: I can drive into town. Might be easier to meet up.

Jack: No. I'll pick you up. Friends do that.

There wasn't any point in arguing about it, so Taylor opted to give in graciously. Especially since it sounded like the whole 'friend' point had finally sunk in.

Taylor: Okay.

Jack paid the dinner bill, but only after using a calculator to figure the tip amount. Taylor had thought him more of a flashy drop the big bucks' kind of guy. Perhaps it was simply a detail-oriented trait, rather than a counting pennies thing.

"You ready to go?" Jack asked, checking his watch.

He hadn't mentioned where else they would go this evening, and she was intrigued by what a man like Jack would do for entertainment. But not enough to give up her penchant for dessert. "I'd like to finish my tiramisu. It's divine."

Jack appeared he wanted to counter her request but simply nodded, his finger tapping the table.

"So, what's the rush? Where are we going next?" Taylor asked, checking out each table in the place. They were in the same restaurant as Randy and Patty, but there'd been no sign of them.

"*Ummm*, I'm taking you home. My plans changed for this evening, and I've got to cut this short."

"Oh, I see." Quite the contrary. Even though she had declared them friends, the idea Jack wanted to dump her off at home as quickly as possible was surprising. "Hot date," she teased, trying to make light of the situation.

"Something like that." He glanced at his watch again.

Enough. This had gone from barely fun to a sudden bore. Talk about an anti-climactic ending. "Okay. We can leave," she said, taking a few more bites and then pushing the plate back.

They rode the short distance to her house in silence. Jack was acting strange, and his eagerness to be rid of her somewhat off-putting. As they pulled up in front of the inn, Jack put the car in park but left the car running.

Talk about a dump and run. "Thanks for dinner," Taylor offered, unwilling to let his rudeness rub off on her.

"No problem. Maybe we can do it again sometime." He put the car in reverse as though to urge her to move along.

She could take a hint. Randy was probably having a way better time with the councilwoman and wouldn't be dropping her off early. At least he wouldn't know the miserable ending to her evening.

"Goodnight," she said, opening the door and sliding out. With a quick wave, she headed toward her cabin. By the time she reached the front door, Jack's taillights were barely visible.

Chapter Fifteen

♥

"Good morning, Dad. How's mother doing?" Taylor asked when her father walked into the kitchen.

"Having a good day and she seems quite encouraged by the doctor's visit yesterday." He moved to the counter by the sink and poured two cups of coffee and added cream to one, just the way her mother liked it.

Music to Taylor's ears, if it meant she could head home early. "Any chance they'll have mom up and moving around without the wheelchair sooner than they thought?"

Her father shrugged and looked away; his attention suddenly focused on the family picture that hung on the wall. "I don't know. Eager to leave us?" he asked.

"Not at all. I love seeing you both. You know I do. It's just that…"

"What is it? You can tell me anything and you know it."

"The thing is I've applied for a new job with a charter company in Alaska. I didn't want to say anything because I didn't even think I would get an interview. But now, I'm in the final candidate selection but it doesn't look like I'll be back in time for the appointment. I've worked hard and deserve the opportunity to show them I'm up to the challenge." Better to tell the truth so that he didn't think her urgency to leave was for any other reason.

"Sweetheart, you have nothing to prove. You are an excellent pilot, and they would be fortunate to have you on the team." Her father had always been her biggest fan. He understood the intricacies of flying and excelled at them.

It would be easier to tell him the truth about her past but couldn't bear to see the light of approval in his eyes fade. "Thanks, Dad. Unfortunately, they won't take my father's opinion as hiring criteria." Taylor shot him a grin, trying to deflect her moment of hesitation to answer.

Her father nodded. "Well, then, their loss is our gain."

"Except I'm not coming home either way. You both know that." They'd been over this before. She needed wings to fly in the sky, but also, personally.

"Not even for Jack? Seems like you two have gone out together a few times, which surprises me. He's not my first choice for you, but seeing as it is your choice, I won't stand in your way. Your mother, now that's another story." He chuckled.

"I can't believe you're counting. I'm not fifteen. And for your information, we're just friends. End of story. And I've told mother the same thing, but no one seems to listen." He wasn't a bad person...just not the right guy for her. But then, hanging out with him twice didn't exactly count for knowing someone since they left high school. "Why is everyone so against him anyway?" Taylor had her reservations, but more because the poor guy seemed like he was trying hard to be the suave, cool guy he portrayed. And why Jack would even want that sort of image was beyond her, but that's not what was in question.

"He just seems...like a tick. Gets under your skin in a bad way. And can you blame us for making the leap when you come home and he's the only guy you spend time with away from here?" And just like that, they had come full circle...back to Randy.

They just never accepted the breakup all those years ago. "I suppose not."

"The guy is just too full of himself."

"Now that is something we agree on." Taylor laughed. It was one of the off-putting qualities she identified early on. Admittedly, it was hard to miss.

Her father paused by the door. "You had me worried when I saw Jack drop you off late last night. Not that your old man was keeping track, mind you."

"Sure, you weren't, Dad. And it was not that late when I got home. Jack had some other place to be, so he dropped me off early."

Her father grinned, the twinkle in his eyes filled with laughter. "Clearly we have different ideas on late."

"Sounds like it. I've got to get started on the strawberry blintz crepes. Would you like me to bring you and mom some to your room when they're finished?" Taylor offered.

"No thanks. Your mother wants to join the guests in the living room for breakfast this morning. She's trying to keep up appearances as an interactive hostess."

Taylor flipped on the pantry light and pulled out the ingredients. She put them on the counter closest to the sink for easier cleanup, knowing the flour would get everywhere. She finished the blintz wraps and then went to work on preparing the filling.

When she was finally ready to cook them, she grabbed the griddle from one of the lower cabinets. Opting to use the side counter since there wasn't much clean room close to the sink, she plugged in the griddle. After setting it for 325 degrees, she moved off to start the clean-up process while it pre-heated.

Minutes passed, and an unfamiliar odor assailed her. Taylor paused, her gaze drifting to the skillet. Nothing appeared out of order. Perhaps it was the oil heating. She didn't use olive oil often when frying because of the lower smoking temperature, but her mother swore by the stuff as the best and healthiest cooking oil.

Taylor finished wiping the counters and putting everything away. The odor was getting stronger, but the oil wasn't smoking. She frowned, trying to figure out the source. It was then she noticed wisps of gray smoke drifting out of the outlet holes.

Something it clearly shouldn't be doing.

She rushed to the skillet and pulled the plug from the outlet. Taylor grabbed the fire extinguisher from under the sink, but there was nothing to spray. Smoke was still pouring out, but there was no fire. A shrill tone emitted from the smoke alarm. Something had to be burning behind the wall.

Her father burst into the room. "What's going on?"

"I think there's a fire behind the wall. It started smoking from the outlet after I plugged in the skillet. There must be a short in the wiring. I'll flip the breaker switch to kill the power."

"Good idea. I'll check the other side. Randy was working on the electrical wiring yesterday and maybe some wires got crossed. We'll call the fire department if we can't isolate the problem and stop it immediately. At least no guests are currently staying in the main house."

Taylor raced to the breaker box in the pantry and flipped the switch, plunging the kitchen into darkness. She pulled out her phone and shook it to activate the flashlight. She lifted the plastic and joined her father in the great room. The smoke was heavier, but worse than that, the wall was on fire. Her father grabbed the fire extinguisher from Taylor and pulled the pin. He sprayed the wall, the white fire-retardant chemical coating the blackened area. Minutes later, they both stood back, hands on hips, to observe the damage and watch for any flare-ups.

Her father let out a heavy sigh, as though the weight of the world was suddenly too much. "I hate to say this, Taylor, but hiring Randy might have been a mistake."

Taylor refused to believe it was Randy's fault. "You don't mean that. He's built an entire business out of what he does because he's good. There must be some other explanation." It was hard to believe she was defending Randy and fighting to keep him on, considering when she first arrived, she wanted him gone. Now was her chance...but not like this. Never, if she was honest.

"Maybe, but that only leaves Dane. And I would fully expect Randy to make sure his employee is fully qualified. I need to fire them. This will break your mother's heart, but I don't know what else to do."

There had to be some way to change her father's mind. "Please, Dad. Don't do anything yet. This job meant a lot to Randy. Let me talk to him. It's always good to get the other side of the story. Something you taught me when I was younger." *Thank you, God.* Her father's words came to mind precisely when needed.

Her father nodded. "Good point. Talk to him and let me know what he says. However, if anything else goes wrong, I won't have any other choice but to fire him. This could have been far worse if we hadn't figured out what was going on so quickly. You handled the situation perfectly, and it was your quick thinking that saved the day." He threw an arm around her shoulder and pulled her close, kissing her forehead, the same way he'd done when she was a child.

Taylor flushed under her father's praise. "I didn't do much. Anyone would know to flip the power off immediately, and you were the one wielding the extinguisher."

"That's not true. You know, you don't take compliments very well. You should just say thank you."

Taylor nodded. He was right; she didn't take compliments well, especially if they were performance related. "Thanks, Dad." It was great that she could remain calm enough to handle a house fire.

But could she handle an engine fire on a plane twenty thousand feet up in the air?

"Looks like I'll be sending the guests into town for breakfast again this morning. This keeps up and we'll have to close the B&B. If word gets around, we're through." Her father's tone sounded bleak, as though he was already resolved to the possibility.

"Then we just need to make sure there's positive publicity about the inn." Taylor couldn't let anything bad happen to the inn. This was her parents' dream. Maybe she should have been home more often. Then she would have known what was happening and been able to help sooner.

"And how do you propose that?"

"I don't know, but I'll think of something." Taylor gave her father a hug. "You better go tell mother so she's not worried."

After her father left, Taylor sat down with a still warm cup of coffee, the smell of smoke lingering in the air. There were just too many accidents for them to be coincidental. But who would want Randy to look bad...maybe even put him out of business?

Jack. The answer came to Taylor like a bolt of lightning, shaking her to the core. He would be the only one who stood to benefit if Randy's current project went up in smoke. *Literally.*

She didn't want to believe Jack would go to such lengths...but what if the leopard hadn't changed his spots? Except last night Jack was with her...at least he was until he wasn't. What if his hot date was with the electrical system at the inn?

And then there was her father's comment about Jack dropping her off late. Had he come back figuring no one would think it odd because she'd gone out with him? It was a suitable cover. All except the dropping her off at eight part. There was no way that could be considered late, even by her father's standards.

Taylor couldn't accuse Jack without proof, but she would pay closer attention. *Even if it meant spending more time with Jack.* He was full of empty flattery, and sometimes when he was with you, he almost seemed like he was someplace else...in his head. She had to know the truth...for Randy's sake.

But what if she was wrong and it was Randy or Dane who really were making the mistakes?

Chapter Sixteen

♥

THE SLAM OF A truck door caught Taylor's attention. She checked her watch and immediately knew it was Randy. Right on time, as usual. But this morning he was in for a rude awakening. She headed outside onto the porch to waylay him, hoping to lessen the shock of the situation.

"Good morning, Randy. Can I have a word with you, please?" She stepped off the porch and headed in his direction.

"Sure. I can afford a few minutes before I get started. We're going to paint the ceiling and walls so that we can lay the flooring tomorrow. It's always exciting to see progress." His good mood wouldn't last through the morning. In fact, it wouldn't last the next ten seconds.

"About that...the progress that is," she paused, trying to find the right words.

Randy's smile faded into a frown. "What's wrong? You're biting your lower lip, something you only do when there's a problem. You've got bad news, haven't you?"

Taylor nodded. "The kitchen wiring caught on fire this morning. The good news is the damage was contained." It was easier to pull the bandage off quickly than to drag out the delivery.

Randy paled, the creases on his forehead like deep ravines. "You've got to be kidding."

"I wish I were."

"Nothing like this ever happens. At this rate, I won't even have a business when I finish this job." Randy started for the side door, Taylor following close behind.

"It's the wall you were working on yesterday. I used the outlet to heat the skillet, and a fire started behind the wall. Dad and I put it out before there was too much damage, but the wiring is fried, and the wall will need to be redone. I'm sorry."

Randy stopped, frowning at her. "It's not your fault, so there's no need for you to apologize." He walked inside and straight to the adjoining wall between the great room and the kitchen. "Son of a gun." He ran a hand through his hair, anger simmering just beneath the surface and threatening to bubble over, tension radiating from every pore of his body. "I don't get it. I handled the wiring personally and I know what I'm doing. This doesn't make any sense." He moved closer.

Taylor felt bad for him, knowing how hard he had been working to get the job done faster...for her. And maybe that was the problem. Was he rushing and therefore it was partly her fault? It was something she had to consider. "Maybe you were distracted," she offered.

"Hardly. Wiring is a serious business. For this very reason," he said, gesturing toward the blackened area. Randy leaned forward for a closer look, using a flashlight to inspect the area. "Well, it's not rocket science to figure out the problem. The wires are crossed. I wouldn't have believed it if I wasn't staring at the evidence firsthand. Clearly, this is my fault. I don't know what's wrong with me lately, but your father needs to find someone else to finish the job before I burn the whole inn down." Randy stood there, shaking his head.

"You don't mean that. The fire damage was kept to a minimum and I'm sure it was just an oversight. We don't expect you to leave," Taylor was quick to point out. Her father had been ready to send Randy packing, but luckily Taylor had convinced him to hold off. Though it didn't help that Randy was taking all the blame. *Again.*

"You should, which is why I quit." Randy moved to pick up some of his tools and laid them by the door.

He was packing up and if she didn't convince him to change his mind, he would simply leave. The thought of him not being there every day was unsettling, but what to say? *Don't go…I'd miss you. Don't go, I might still love you. Or don't go, I need you.*

None of which sounded right.

"You can't quit," her father said, joining them. "You promised to get this finished by next week, and I'm holding you to it. But no more mistakes…please," his tone borderline desperate.

Randy let out a deep sigh. "I'm sorry about all this. You can't possibly want me to keep working here. I appreciate the vote of confidence, and honestly, at this point, I can't promise nothing else will go wrong."

"Just try, son. That's all I can ask of you. Taylor believes in you, and therefore, so do we."

Randy swiveled to face her, a questioning expression on his face.

One she didn't want to answer. She couldn't believe her father had hinted at what she said earlier. Taylor nodded, unwilling to explain.

He turned back to her father. "I did promise and if you're not firing me, then I should be grateful and finish the project. I'll get here first every morning and leave last every day, just to recheck the daily work. Thank you, sir."

Except Taylor knew it was the same mode of operation he already had in place.

"You're welcome. And it sounds like an excellent plan," her father said, before turning and walking back out the way he had come. His timing had been perfect. Almost too perfect, as if he too had been waiting to have a word with Randy.

Taylor had beaten him to it, but she was grateful for his interference. All except the comment where he all but said Taylor was one of Randy's biggest fans. She couldn't imagine what Randy was thinking at this point with that information.

And Taylor finally understood why she was trying so hard to make things right with Randy. *She still loved him*. Even if the only person she could admit it to was herself. It changed nothing...their futures were not on the same path. But the heart didn't understand logistics...only emotions. That and the fact she was the one who wrongfully broke things off years ago, and she owed him big time.

One thing was for certain...there were too many coincidences not adding up with all the mishaps. It was time to put her plan into motion.

Operation Truth.

Jack was her prime…and only suspect, and that's where she would start. She fired off a text asking him to meet her for lunch. His prompt acceptance was almost a surprise given his hot date with someone else last night. But then, if she was right, his hot date wasn't a woman…it had been a date with foul play.

Jack's sharp rap on the front door announced his arrival. Taylor grabbed her purse and headed for the porch, hoping to avoid Randy and her parents, not wanting to deal with their disapproving gazes. Randy and Jack weren't friends, not by a long shot, and it would be best to avoid any chance meeting.

"Good afternoon. I'm so glad you were free," Taylor said, coating her words with a sweetness she wasn't feeling. If her instincts were right, Jack was more like a skunk.

"For you…anytime," Jack said, taking her by the arm and leading her towards his flashy red Mercedes.

"Except last night," she teased, pleased at how easily the subject came up.

"Last night was an exception. Sorry…but if it makes you feel better, it was business, not pleasure."

Hint number one that might confirm her theory. It was a stretch, but… "Oh. Well, in that case." She grinned at him. The real question came with a twist. Was it a behind the scenes dirty dealing business? "A new female client, no doubt. I know you, Jack Tinsdale."

He chuckled as he opened her door, allowing Taylor to slide into the passenger seat. "You almost sound jealous. Which isn't something I expect, but definitely like. It gives me hope you might fall for me yet."

Hardly. "Maybe. So, was she pretty?"

Jack slid into the driver's seat. "Who?"

"The client last night," she pressed.

Jack's smile deepened as he laid a hand across hers and squeezed. "Taylor, relax. You've got this all wrong. There was no client last night. Just some unfinished business that needed to be handled. You would certainly keep me on my toes if you were my girlfriend."

Never going to happen. "Good. I mean, that there wasn't a hot date with another woman. Not about being your girlfriend. We've already settled that." *Thank goodness.*

"I see Randy's here this morning. He must be about done the repairs?" Jack asked, turning to face her, his gaze lingering on her face.

Her imagination jumped to the conclusion his gaze was almost too watchful. She'd make a terrible sleuth. "Nearly. Another week, tops." The job might have been already done if it weren't for all the setbacks that kept happening.

"That's good. I heard in town he's had a few mishaps. Never good for business or finishing a project on time." A leading question to find out what was really happening behind the scenes at the inn?

Information Taylor had no intention of sharing. "He and Dane have been putting in some extra hours to stay on track. They are hard workers, and they do such good work. My parents love their attention to detail."

Jack scowled ever so briefly before he forced a smile back in place. "Well, that's good then. No more mishaps I reckon," Jack said, one eyebrow quirked upward.

She couldn't tell if it was a statement or a question. "None, thankfully," she lied. If Jack slipped up and mentioned the electrical fire, she'd have him dead to rights since no one knew except her, her father, and Randy.

Taylor peered around the interior of the car, looking for clues but trying not to look obvious. "I like your Mercedes. I don't know how you keep it so clean."

"Image is everything in my business. I take it to First Class Auto Care every Thursday for a complete wash, wax, and interior cleaning. Just had it done this morning."

"That's why it smells so nice. I always do my own wash, vacuum, and clean to save money." Especially on something she could easily do herself.

Jack shrugged. "Leaves time for business...and making the money to pay for someone else to do services like that." He laughed at his own joke while Taylor still viewed it as unnecessary and certainly not funny worthy.

Her phone rang as they pulled up to the diner. "Hey, Dad. What's up?"

"Where are you? Your mother is having a rough morning, and she wants your help so she can take a shower."

Taylor glanced at Jack. "I'm sorry. I was about to have lunch with a friend, but I can come home."

"If you don't mind, dear. She seems a bit put out about something, and I never told her about the kitchen fire, so I don't know what's wrong."

Taylor had her suspicions. Most likely, her mother saw her leave with Jack. "No problem, Dad. I'll be right there."

"Sorry, Jack. I've got to get back to the inn. My mother's not having a good morning and since I came home to help, I need to get back. Maybe we can do this some other time."

Jack nodded, his smile slipping. "I understand, but perhaps you can promise me dinner and dancing this weekend to make it up. I'm hoping to have a new contract to celebrate. This will be a huge feather in my cap if I can land the deal."

"I'll see what I can do." Taylor smiled, but deep down, she already knew her answer. No way. *Unless it would help Randy.*

Ten minutes later, Jack dropped her off at the main house. Taylor went in search of her mother, but she was nowhere to be found. She went outside and spotted Randy. "Hey, have you seen my mother?"

"She was here about fifteen minutes ago, but then she headed for the barn. She's trucking right along in the motorized wheelchair, so there's no telling where she might be now."

Taylor frowned, her assessment of her mother's urgent request spot on. "So not a shower," she muttered out loud.

"I don't understand," Randy said, suddenly confused.

"Never mind. It's nothing. My father called and said I was needed back here right away. Looks like he was wrong, is all."

Randy grinned. "Oh, that's too bad. It's a shame you had to cut your date short with Jack. Not sure what you see in the guy." He didn't seem at all sorry the date ended practically from the start.

Taylor wanted to tell Randy her suspicions, but knew it wasn't the right thing to do. It might be nice to figure this out together, like a team. But he was too involved in the outcome if she was right in her suspicions, and it wouldn't look good if he was the one calling foul play. This was something she needed to investigate on her own in case she was wrong. "He can be nice enough."

"Nice as a snake," he mumbled, but Taylor heard him.

She wholeheartedly agreed. "Spoken like a true competitor," she teased, hoping to deflect the conversation to safer territory.

"There won't be a competition between us if things keep going wrong on this job site. Guess I should focus on my job and let you focus on your boyfriend." Randy's tone of disapproval shocked her to the core.

"He's not my boyfriend," Taylor huffed and walked away, unwilling to discuss Jack...least of all with Randy.

The man who confused her to no end. The same man she had loved since she was sixteen and apparently had never stopped loving.

.

Chapter Seventeen

♥

AFTER DINNER, TAYLOR WANTED nothing more than to head for her cabin and relax. She tapped on her mother's bedroom door to see if she needed anything else for the evening. Taylor was still a little vague on the miscommunication this afternoon that prevented her from lunching with Jack, but in the end, was a good near miss.

Her mother didn't answer, and Taylor knocked again, this time pushing the door slightly ajar to see inside, hoping she was okay. The sight of her mom coming out of the bathroom was shocking, given that she was moving about without crutches. Her mother's guilt-ridden expression said a lot. The wheelchair in the corner of the room was the rest of the story. "Mother!"

"Oh, dear. I can explain. I thought you had already left for the night." Her mother pulled her robe tight and cinched the tie, then grabbed the pair of crutches by the door and hobbled over to the bed.

"Clearly. What's up with the crutches? And how long have you been using them?"

Her mother sat on the bed, laying them next to her. "I tested walking around and seemed to do okay. I've been getting stronger every day. The doctor said it was fine."

Taylor frowned. "That's not the point. How long have you been *testing*? You certainly don't seem like a beginner. And when were you going to tell me about this?" If her mother could get around the kitchen with crutches, a walker with a basket would enable her to do most of the kitchen work, provided her father chipped in and helped.

"I was going to tell you tomorrow. The doctor thought I should start moving around more and that I was ready. Your father and I just wanted you to stay a few more days until we saw how this would work out. It's been so wonderful having you home for a visit, dear. We never see you except on the computer with that video call thing."

Her mother was laying the guilt on thick again. "Except that's not your only reason, and we both know it."

She had the good graces to look apologetic. "Is it so wrong for me to want to see you happy? The way you were before you left home? Before things ended with Randy. And when I spoke to him about what you told me, he was shocked. That man has never stopped loving you."

"Enough. You've got to let go of this idea that Randy and I should be together. I don't even live in North Carolina. And yes, I know all about you telling him what I said, which I don't appreciate. But I forgive you. In the end, it was good to clear the air between us. I'm thrilled, however, that you're doing better because now I can go home and get on with my life." She'd already missed the interview window with the charter company, but she still had her own job to do. "If you want my happiness, then let me sort out my own life...without interference. You tricked me, so I'd stay longer. This is beyond anything I expected from you. Does Dad know?" Taylor was frustrated with her mother but couldn't bring herself to be mad. Maybe irritated was a good word...but she loved her mother and wouldn't stay irritated with her for long. Based on history, it would last five minutes.

Her mother nodded. "Yes, dear. I'm sorry. He didn't want to go along with my plan, but he did it for me. Don't blame him." It explained some of her father's comments, but as always, mother always got her way.

"Can you stay a few more days? Help me change back to a full schedule? Please, Taylor."

"Fine. But just a few days, Mother." She dropped a kiss on her cheek and headed out the door. It's not like it would change the interview outcome anyway.

It was a beautiful, warm evening as the sun set, lighting up the skies in brilliant shades of orange and red, streaking behind the billowing clouds. Taylor headed for the cabin, noticing Randy's truck was still parked outside. The man was dedicated to getting the job done, despite all the setbacks. And true to his word, he was going to stick around and be the last person on the job site at night.

Taylor poured a glass of iced tea and sat down on the front porch, hoping to catch sight of the elk. So far, the magnificent beast hadn't been back around. Taylor's phone vibrated, a west coast area code popping up with a strange number.

Curious, she pressed the answer button. "Taylor Thompson."

"Hello, Ms. Thompson. My name is Brian Sanders, and I'm one of the directors with Alaskan Adventures. I've talked with Bob Chandler at length about the candidates, and you are most certainly one of our top contenders for the position. I understand you're on the east coast on a family business matter, but if anything has changed, I'd still like you to come in for an interview. I can extend the offer through tomorrow if you can fly out here. If you're still interested in the position, that is. You have quite the resume and I feel you might very well be the valuable member of the team we are looking for. We just need to put you through the flight paces, as I'm sure you understand."

Taylor swallowed, her throat dry and her heart racing, fear and adrenaline coursing through her body, threatening to consume her. "I'm still very interested and I understand the need for a first-hand review process. I truly appreciate the extension. It's just that I'm not sure when I can leave." A picture of her mother moving about on crutches flashed in front of her. Maybe she could make the interview after all.

"I'm sorry to hear that. We simply can't hold the spot open forever."

Taylor wanted the job, but she was also scared. The flight test was almost enough for her to close the door on the job once and for all, but she couldn't do it. This was the opportunity she'd been waiting for in order to prove to herself she was an excellent pilot. "Wait. I can fly home tomorrow morning early and meet with you in the afternoon since the time-zone gains me three hours." Her mother wouldn't be happy about the change in plans, but this was Taylor's future. And she didn't feel the slightest bit guilty about leaving, not after the stunt her mother pulled.

Taylor finished packing and knew it was time to head to the main house to break the news to her parents, hoping they were still awake. Randy's truck was still parked out front, which was surprising given it was almost nine PM. There was dedication to one's job, and then there was too much dedication. Fourteen hours on site would certainly make anyone prone to mistakes. This was the second time the idea crossed her mind. Doubts plagued her again, whether she was on a wild goose chase to find a reason for the problems that kept popping up to protect Randy.

Unfortunately, she doubted herself. It was a good thing she'd kept quiet and not blasted a man's reputation without proof. Decision made, she veered right and headed for the side entrance. It would give her the opportunity to let Randy know she was leaving town. Stepping inside the great room, she looked around but didn't see or hear him. "Hello, anyone here?" she called out, heading for the kitchen.

There was no answer, and she lifted the plastic sheeting to step into the kitchen. There was still no sign of Randy. She moved back into the great room and turned to leave, wondering if she had missed him outside.

Taylor pulled the door open and started forward, but stopped, a low groan like an injured wild animal alarming her. She hesitated before stepping back inside. It was then she heard the sound again, this time, clearly coming from the far corner of the room. Taylor spun around, noticing the basement door was ajar.

She pulled open the door. "Randy?" she called into the dark recesses. It wouldn't make sense for anyone to be in the basement without a light on. The low moan sounded again. Taylor flipped on the light and started down the stairs, pausing at the sight of a body lying at the bottom of the stairs like a rag doll.

"Randy!" she screamed, jogging down the last steps. His low groan meant he was alive, but it sucked the life from Taylor as she tried to figure out what to do. Her heart raced as her medical training rushed in to rescue her from indecision. Checking him over, his pulse was erratic but strong, and his breathing labored. No bones seemed obviously out of place or at odd angles. It was the wound on his head that worried her most. Blood had pooled onto the floor, and Taylor quickly inspected the area, trying to spot something she could use to stop the bleeding.

Taylor grabbed a sheet off the washing machine and ripped it into usable pieces, then wrapped it around Randy's head. With any luck, the bleeding would stop.

"Randy, can you hear me? It's Taylor. You fell down the stairs. I'm going to call for help."

"Pushed." The single, yet barely a whisper word, held a wealth of meaning. She must have misunderstood him.

Taylor pulled her phone out and dialed 911.

"911 Dispatch. What's your emergency?" The woman's soothing voice was like a much-needed balm to Taylor's nerves.

"I need an ambulance. Stat. A man fell down the concrete stairs and has a head wound. He's not moving, but alive. I've wrapped a sheet around his head to restrict the bleeding. Hurry." Taylor rattled off the address, and the woman assured her a medical team would be there in less than ten minutes.

"An ambulance is on the way. Hang in there, Randy," Taylor said, unable to keep the tears from falling. He couldn't die. Not now. Not like this.

"Pushed," he said again, as though the very effort cost him.

There was no way she misunderstood him a second time, but there was no one else there. It didn't make any sense. "Don't move," she said, cradling his head better when it rolled to one side.

Taylor checked for a pulse and was relieved to feel his heartbeat, even if it was faint and slow. The wail of sirens filled the air, a welcoming sound as Taylor sat with Randy, praying he would be alright.

"Taylor?" her father called out from the kitchen.

"I'm in the basement, Dad. With Randy. Send the paramedics down here." Having her father near was the dose of calming Taylor needed. It wasn't just her fighting to save Randy...there would be others in a matter of seconds.

He was at the top of the stairs, quickly taking stock of the situation. "I'm on it," he said and then turned to leave, fully grasping the situation.

Taylor was grateful the paramedics had arrived. Within seconds, medical personnel rushed down the stairs and she stepped back to give them access. She repeated everything she knew, answering their questions to the best of her ability. "Will he be okay?" she asked.

"God willing," the paramedic said. "I'm sorry to have to tell you this, but he's completely unresponsive now and his vitals support a possible coma status. Sometimes the brain does this as a means of protection. We need to get him to a high-level ER center to have this properly diagnosed and to get him the emergency treatment he needs. I'm calling in for a medical airlift."

The two men moved Randy onto a stretcher, and then the man who had spoken placed a call. He hung up shortly after. "Bad news. The helicopter is already responding to another call. We've got to get him stabilized for the next forty-five minutes to an hour before they can get here."

"Where were you taking him?" Taylor asked.

"To Meyer's Medical in Asheville."

"What about Stanton Hospital in Raleigh? I can fly Randy there if one of you can go with me to monitor his condition. We can be there before the helicopter has even the slightest chance of arriving. I fly charter flights and am licensed for medical transport. My best friend should be working in the emergency room tonight. I can make sure they are ready and waiting. The landing strip is big enough for my small two-engine plane, unlike the Meyer's facility, which can only handle the helicopters." She was talking fast, but Taylor needed them to agree...for Randy's sake.

The paramedic shook his head. "I'm sorry. It's not really protocol."

"But you said yourself that time was of the essence," Taylor said, her voice rising on the edge of hysteria. "We have to do something. You can't just let him die."

"My daughter knows what she's doing, and she's right. It's the best chance you've got for this young man to survive," her father said, stepping forward, placing one hand on her shoulder to offer moral support.

The two men were silent for a moment. The paramedic in charge finally nodded. "Fine. Let me call it in and get approval. My name's Tony by the way. And I'll need to see your license to cover our butts on liability. But I reckon you can consider yourself on the job. You best see to your plane, and we'll get this gentleman loaded on board. Let's roll everyone. This man's life is in our hands."

In God's hands. *Please Lord, help me save Randy. I need You with me now more than ever. Steady my mind and fill me with the peace that only You can provide.*

Chapter Eighteen

♥

TAYLOR RACED TO THE cabin and grabbed her purse. By the time she returned, they had moved Randy on the stretcher to the great room. His lifeless body was a heart wrenching sight that broke her heart. She shook off the emotional vice grip that held her in place, knowing this wasn't the time to give in to her fear. She handed the paramedic both her pilot's license and her medical certification.

"I'm going to go run a quick pre-flight check, warm up the engines, and call in a flight plan. My father will show you the way to the airstrip on our property."

"Thanks for doing this. This guy must be pretty special to you and one day soon he'll have his guardian angel to thank for saving his life."

Taylor clung to the ray of hope the older man offered with his comment and gentle smile. "Thank me when this is over and it all goes well."

"Be careful, Taylor. We'll be praying for Randy...and you," her mother said, moving close to hug her.

Taylor didn't know when she arrived on the scene, but she was comforted by her presence. "Thanks, Mom."

"You'll be fine, sweetheart. Have a safe flight and please update us as soon as you can," her father said.

"Thanks, Dad. I will." Taylor rushed out of the room, as much to keep her from getting sucked into the emotional heartache of seeing the love of her life fight for his life, as to be the one to help him make it happen. Everything and everyone were counting on her.

Less than five minutes later, Taylor had clearance for a Medevac priority flight to Stanton hospital in Raleigh. TRACON would clear the airspace at 15,000 feet momentarily. She said a prayer of gratitude Sandy was on duty and would mobilize the medical team to be ready for their arrival at the hospital's landing area twenty-six minutes after she had the Piper in the air. There, an ambulance would be waiting to transport him to the emergency room three minutes away.

Taylor's deepest fears threatened to engulf her, but she held them at bay...for Randy's sake. She ran through a minimal pre-flight checklist to have them in the air and on their way. *Minutes counted in a flight for life.*

She fired up the engines, the loud roar satisfying. It wouldn't be long, and they'd be airborne. Taylor ran a last check on the instrument panel, testing the wing flaps and rechecking the instrument panel. The two paramedics arrived in the ambulance, lights flashing. They parked close to the steps, and then the two paramedics lifted Randy on the stretcher and carried him inside the cabin. Space was tight based on seating, but luckily, she was set for charters which had minimal seating to allow for cargo transport as well. And Taylor had removed the two back seats to make room for a specialized medical transport area. Over the years, she'd had only a handful of medical transports...and none this critical. Or someone she knew...and loved.

"You about ready? We're all set here," the paramedic said as he finished locking the stretcher into place on the gurney which was also attached to the plane itself. "I'll be traveling with you to monitor the patient."

"Sounds good. I'm ready to roll. No change with Randy?" Taylor asked, wishing she could be with him. Except she had a more important job to do...fly the plane.

The man shook his head. "None. Sorry."

"The hospital is expecting us in thirty minutes so let's get airborne."

"Gotcha." Tony took a seat closest to Randy and buckled himself in, Taylor's signal to return to the cockpit.

She checked the instrument panel one last time, and then adjusted the flaps to the proper angle for takeoff and performed a run-up the engines. It was dark outside, but the lights from the plane guided her as she pushed in the fuel mixture knob and advanced the throttle slowly to generate thrust, moving her forward until it was full open and she was up to speed for takeoff, the plane bumping along the runway, then she pulled back on the yoke to lift the front of the plane. In minutes, they were airborne and circling back to the east for the flight.

Everything had gone off perfectly, and she breathed a sigh of relief. She pinpointed the landing area for the hospital on the radar and made a straight path for it as she continued to climb in altitude. "TRACON, this is November 3-1-2 Mike Tango. We are airborne and twenty-one minutes from SL Tower. Cruising altitude at 15,000 feet and holding."

"Roger. Cleared to SL Tower N312MT."

Taylor couldn't help but look back into the cabin, hoping to see Randy moving around. Taylor said another prayer, knowing it was the only other thing she could do at this point.

The hospital location started blinking on her screen. She picked up her phone and called Sandy. Her friend answered on the first ring. "I'm on schedule and ten minutes out, Sandy."

"See you soon. Don't worry, Taylor. Some of the best doctors in the country work here. We'll find out what's going on and then deal with whatever comes our way. Just keep the faith."

"I am. Trust me. It's all I'm running on now." Taylor hung up, her focus on her approach. Just a few more minutes and she'd start her descent. A quick check showed everything in order for the landing. She flipped the switch to lower her landing gear. Keeping the wings level, she moved into position for the landing after getting radio tower clearance.

The plane shook a bit, an alarm sounding a second later on the instrument panel. The plane started to yaw and roll. She tested both pedals for directional turning, but the right one did nothing, indicating the right engine was not responding. Taylor scanned the gauges as the light and alarm sounded off for the right engine. Spitting and sputtering, the plane drifted to the right, without the full power of both engines to hold it steady. Taylor swallowed hard. It came on fast and was acting like there was a fuel issue. Adrenaline coursed through her veins, understanding the dangers of trying to land a plane with one functional engine. There wasn't time to rationalize why there was a problem, only to figure out a way to land safely. She lowered the nose to gain air speed and reduced power on the good engine.

"Mayday. Mayday. Mayday. SL Tower. This is November 3-1-2 Mike Tango. I've got engine trouble. Possible fuel issues."

The radio crackled to life. "N312MT. Roger. I see you are on descent. Can you land the plane?" the faceless man asked.

The right engine shut down completely, the plane lurching to the right with it now under only one engine. "Update SL Tower. The right engine shut off completely. The left engine appears fine. Possible fuel starvation. And I have no idea if I can land the plane, but do I have any other choice?"

"No, you don't. I'm going to have the air space cleared around SL Tower. I'm a pilot and understand what you are facing. I'll stay with you and talk you through the landing. Firetrucks have been dispatched and will meet you on the airstrip."

"Roger SL Tower. I've done this many times in simulation successfully, but I appreciate the assist." *Except once, that is.* This was her worst nightmare come true. *Engine failure.*

It was even the same engine that failed. How twisted was fate? Or was God giving her the chance to move past her fears and get it right? Because this time, it wasn't a test…it was for real. And it wasn't just her life on the line, but two innocent passengers. One of them the man she loved.

Taylor shoved every other thought out of her head except the important one. Keeping the plane level…a feat made almost impossible without two engines to equalize the effort. The plane was losing altitude and as much as she would have liked to pass over the airstrip and regroup to try from a different angle; she didn't have time. There simply wasn't enough power to climb in altitude.

She flipped on the switch for automatic cabin audio. "Bad news, Tony. I've lost power on one engine. We're in for a rough landing. You've got about sixty seconds to take a seat and put on your seatbelt." There wouldn't be an answer, but she knew he could hear her and prayed he followed her directions.

The airstrip was in sight, flashing red lights lining the short landing strip. It was like landing a bull in an arena…unleashed power waiting to crush anyone not at the top of their game.

Please, Lord. Taylor struggled to keep the plane level, as it yawed and rolled. The air traffic controller continued to speak to her through the headset, encouraging her and giving instructions.

So close. The plane bounced on the tarmac and veered right. Without both engines, there was no way to easily steer the plane down the runway. She pumped the brakes to slow the plane down, sending it into a spin.

Seconds felt like hours. Taylor applied the brakes more firmly as the wheels settled on the tarmac. The plane finally came to a stop, and she couldn't stop the tears from pouring down her face. She'd landed the plane. They were all safe. *Randy was safe.*

Thank you, Lord.

"Good job, N 312MT. Now get everyone out of the plane. ASAP."

"Roger SL Tower. And thanks for the assist."

Taylor unbuckled her restraints and charged into the cabin. "Are you both okay?"

"Right as rain. That was some pretty fancy dancing you did with the plane. Holy smokes!" Tony grinned as he stood up and checked on Randy, the man also on an adrenaline high, knowing they'd survived an emergency landing.

"We've got to get out of the plane in case there's a fire." Taylor rushed to unlock the door and lower the steps.

The fire trucks surrounded the plane, and an ambulance rushed to greet them. Sandy jumped out and headed her way.

"Wow. Nice work, Ace. You can tell me about that landing later. But we've got to get Randy into the ER. Stat." Sandy gave her a quick hug, but then rushed inside the plane with the medical team.

"I did it," she squeaked out, though she was the only one left standing there. She was still afraid to believe it was true. It was over...and she'd done what she needed to do in an emergency. Her heart rejoiced, but only for a few seconds as she watched them carry Randy down the steps.

None of what she did mattered if Randy didn't make it. *Please, Lord. Help make him well. He means the world to me. I love him with all my heart and soul.*

It didn't change anything between them because they still had two different lives, but he just had to be okay.

She couldn't ask him to give up his business and move to California any more than he could ask her to do the same and move back to North Carolina.

Her heart would forever be with him, but for right now, she wouldn't leave until she knew he was going to be okay. There were some things more important than job interviews and Randy fit the bill...*even if she couldn't tell him.*

Chapter Nineteen

♥

For the past two days, Taylor stayed with Sandy at her apartment. She was grateful for her best friend's encouraging words and prayers. It had been a tense thirty-six hours, but the doctor now believed Randy would come out of the coma. Time was a magical healer for the brain...or so he said. Taylor believed God was watching over Randy.

Taylor's mother had stepped back into her role as manager at the inn, her father filling in the gaps. It would seem they were managing without her, just as she suspected they would if Taylor had flown back to San Francisco. Of course, her mother's spirits had improved now that she was back on her feet and mingling with guests...even if she had to hobble along on crutches.

Taylor also knew why her mother insisted she stay in Raleigh to be with Randy. Her mother was a glass-half-full kind of person, and she wanted this time to magically fix all the issues between them, hoping to gain a son-a-law, and have her daughter come home...for good.

It wasn't at her mother's urging that she stayed by Randy's bedside, alternating with his parents as they stood by helplessly watching their son fight for his life. She stayed because of her love for him.

For hours, she listened to the never-ending beeps and whirring of the machines but didn't mind as they were a source of reassurance. So was reading the Bible. She read stories and passages to Randy, hoping he could hear her. Maybe even recognize her voice and come back. *To her.*

Wishful thinking. Those days were long gone.

She never heard from the charter company, but then Taylor couldn't blame them. The interview had been the last of her worries from the moment she discovered Randy at the bottom of the steps. With so much on her mind, she hadn't even sent them an email to apologize for not showing up. Not that it mattered. Mr. Sanders had been clear it was her last chance and that they couldn't hold the position open forever. After all, they had a company to run.

Taylor moved to Randy's side and lifted his hand, holding it close to her heart. "Come back to me, Randy.

Please," she said, her voice soft, urging him to sense her presence.

His hand tightened ever so slightly on hers. Was she imagining things? "Randy?"

He repeated the move, proving he could hear her voice and that it wasn't Taylor's imagination.

Taylor said a prayer of thanks, and the second she finished, Randy's eyes fluttered open, then closed. He squinted as though the lights were too bright. Taylor pressed the call button to alert the staff and then raced to dim the room's light. It was a truly magical moment she would never forget.

The nurse came in. "What's—"

"He's waking up. He opened his eyes and looked right at me. I think the lights were too bright." She moved back to the bedside, willing Randy to open his eyes again.

The nurse beamed. "That's wonderful. I'll get the doctor and be right back." She hurried out of the room, the door closing behind her.

Taylor smiled as tears of joy ran unchecked. He opened his eyes again...and smiled. *At her.*

She rubbed the tears away that were blurring her vision. "Hey there, glad to have you back with us."

"Wha—" he started to say, then stopped. One hand went to his head, touching the bandage still wrapped there. "What happened?" he asked.

"You fell down the basement stairs and cracked your head. Gave me quite the scare."

He frowned, rubbing his temples. "I fell? That doesn't sound right." Randy tried to sit up but fell back against the pillow as he glanced at the tubing and wires attached to his body, and then at the machine they were connected to.

"Don't worry about anything right now, Randy…just get well. We can sort this all out later." She laid a hand on his arm, hoping to soothe some of the confused tension away. It would be difficult waking up and finding yourself in a hospital, especially given the circumstances.

"How long have I been here?" he asked, resignation in his voice.

"Well, we got here Thursday night, and it's Saturday afternoon."

"Where's here?"

"Stanton Hospital. In Raleigh." Taylor wasn't sure how much she should tell him. What if it was too much stress, and he relapsed? She prayed the doctor would arrive soon.

"How did I get here? I don't remember much of anything."

"I flew you here in my plane." She looked toward the door, wishing the doctor or nurse would return.

"You did? Why?"

"Maybe you should ask the doctor," she said, unsure of how to answer the question.

"Taylor, clearly something happened. And clearly, you know what. So, spill."

She didn't like to see him getting agitated and the doctor still hadn't arrived, leaving her no choice. "Fine, but please don't worry about anything other than getting better...and out of the hospital."

"Taylor..."

"You needed a Medevac. You fell down the stairs and were knocked unconscious. I was the best way for you to get urgent medical care."

"Sounds like a nutshell version, but I'll take it. And thank you." Randy's eyes drifted shut, as though he was tired. The door pushed open, and he turned his head to see who had arrived.

The doctor moved next to Randy's bedside. "Welcome back, young man."

"Thanks," Randy said, shifting to get more comfortable but the effort seemed to cost him.

The doctor checked the machine and then jotted down some notes on the medical clipboard attached to the bed. "Everything is looking good. We need to run a few tests, but I think it's safe to say you are in the clear. You gave your girlfriend quite a scare."

"I'm not—"

"Really?" Randy's questioning expression caused Taylor to squirm.

"Absolutely. She's been here most of the time, just sitting and reading to you. She's a keeper, son." The kindly doctor had no clue of the emotional battlefield he had stepped into.

Taylor shook her head but didn't have the heart to contradict the doctor's fairytale spin on their relationship. It's not like Randy didn't know the truth.

"I couldn't agree more," Randy said, a hint of a grin appearing.

Or not. Perhaps the fall had damaged the memory area of his brain.

"Taylor, this would be a good time for you to take a rest. We need to run some tests and then let him sleep some more. Maybe you could come back this evening now that you've seen he's out of the woods."

Taylor nodded. "Okay. I'll call your parents with the good news. They've been here as well. When I get back, you and I can talk more. I'm thinking your memory has shorted out." She grinned, more than relieved to have Randy awake enough to tease her.

"Thanks for being here for me."

"You're welcome. Maybe if you fully cooperate with the doctor, you can spring from this joint and I can give you a lift home soon." Taylor shot him a wink. Of course, she'd have to get the engine repaired and run several test flights before that could happen. Luckily, her parents had the foresight to come in two cars when they visited, leaving one of them for Taylor to use.

"Sounds like a plan. And Taylor," Randy said, stopping her when she reached the door. "I didn't fall. I was pushed."

Taylor sucked in a deep breath. It was the same thing he'd told her the night of the accident before he had slipped into a coma. "We'll deal with that later. Right now, we all need you to get better." It wouldn't do any good to worry him more than necessary. But it also wouldn't stop her from doing what she needed to do. Find out what really happened that night...if she could.

And the first thing she needed to do was return to the inn to investigate the scene where he fell. After all, Taylor already suspected someone was trying to discredit Randy's work. Sabotage his work was more like it. And she only had one suspect.

But would Jack go so far as trying to kill Randy for the historical contract?

Taylor was lucky enough to have a friend of Sandy's offer to fly her to Moonridge. It was a quick flight...way better than the four hours it would take to drive. Her father was meeting her at the private airport not far from the B&B to drive her back to the house as the plane was too big to land on their own runway.

Lost in a sea of thoughts, Taylor missed the beauty of the flight. Something she never did, so it was surprising to realize they were landing.

"Thanks for doing this, Stan. I really appreciate your help."

"All good. Gives me a chance to visit some friends and catch a hike. The views are spectacular here in the Smokies," Stan said, as he lowered the steps, and allowed her to exit the plane. "See you at six," he added.

Her father was waiting, right on schedule. "Good to see you again, Taylor. Wonderful news about Randy. Your mother has been in prayer warrior mode and your text message he woke up was such a blessing."

"I would have called but decided it would be easier to catch you up in person. Thanks for picking me up." The warmth of his bear hug was exactly what Taylor needed. Someone to lean on, and in times like now, it felt good to give over her emotions and let someone else be in control.

"When are you headed back to the hospital?"

"In a couple of hours. Stan, the pilot who flew me here, is going on a short hike with some friends and we are meeting back here at six. I just needed to pick up some clothes and take care of a few things." It wouldn't do well to tell her father her suspicions. Time enough for that if she was right. Though in this case, she would rather be wrong.

"Well, make sure you talk to your mother before you head back. A friend came and picked her up to take her into town. She shouldn't be gone long, and I know she's looking forward to seeing you."

"I will. Hopefully, she's back before I need to leave."

Her father nodded. "I reckon it's none of my business, but I can't help but want to butt in. Father's prerogative of sorts." They headed for his truck.

"What's going on?" Taylor wondered if he too had suspicions about the so-called accidents.

"Calling it like I see it, but whether you want to admit it or not, you still love Randy. So why fight it? I mean, it's not like everyone can't see the truth."

Taylor shook her head. "It's not that simple, Dad. Things happened in the past between Randy and I, and even though we've since laid some of those issues to rest, the fact remains...we are two different people now. I've got a life in San Francisco and Randy's is here. Maybe love isn't enough." Who was she trying to convince? *Her father...or herself.*

"You know, sometimes the path you choose in life isn't the right one. Perhaps you should pray about it and God will help you discover the answers you aren't even sure you're looking for."

"Dad..." Her father didn't have emotional discussions often, and Taylor heard what he was saying. *What if he was right?* She liked her life...but what if it could have been better? The road not taken...where would it have left her? With Randy...in Moonridge. Who knows...maybe she wouldn't have finished college. Or gotten her pilot's license. Maybe she'd be a mother by now. The choices were limitless, but they weren't reality.

Parents didn't always understand, and this was one of those times. After missing the interview, the thought of what to do next or where she could apply tinkered in the dim recesses of her brain. Charter piloting wasn't the type of job that became available every day. But what she believed wholeheartedly was that the job was never meant to be hers. Too many obstacles made that point quite clear. God's plan for her life didn't include the Alaskan Adventures. The good news was that even without the charter company, Taylor now firmly believed in herself and her abilities as a pilot.

The sky was the limit...truly applied.

Her father pulled up to the front door of the inn. "I've got to run to the barn and then to drop off some fresh linens and towels at Wolf cabin. See you soon, sweetheart."

Taylor slid out of the truck and waved as her father drove off. She started toward her cabin, then changed her mind. Better to get this part of her trip over with first, without prying eyes questioning her motive. Not that she knew what she was looking for, but anything out of the ordinary was a good place to search.

There was nothing obvious by the door, no signs of forced entry, nothing that jumped out at her to send up a warning flag. She moved inside, sucking in a deep breath, trying to quell the rising panic. She wasn't sure how long she would last at this rate, deciding to face the stairs to the basement first…before she lost her nerve.

Flipping on the light, she steeled herself for the emotional reaction. To her surprise, nothing seemed much different. Until she reached the bottom of the stairs and spotted traces of blood. Her stomach did a flip-flop and nausea settled in. She turned away, searching the area for anything out of the ordinary.

Except there wasn't anything, and she was no closer to knowing what happened Thursday night.

Taylor headed back up the stairs, eager to be away from the musty basement and the memories that assailed her. She flipped off the light and closed the door, moving back into the main room. She stood there, scanning the area. With nothing out of place, she turned to leave. Her gaze caught on a tiny but bright yellow piece of paper under the area where excess plastic lay wadded up on the floor.

Bending over, she picked up the ticket. There was nothing on it and she flipped it over to inspect the other side. There were four words, a number, and a date stamp. Four very important words. *First Class Car Care*. And it was dated Thursday, the same day Jack had his car cleaned before he picked her up.

Was it possible this was Jack's receipt, and he had dropped it here by accident? Taylor frowned, understanding the importance of what she held if it were in fact, Jack's receipt. When he had come to pick her up, they had met on the porch and left right away. He had never been in the house.

Which could only mean one thing...if it was Jack...he'd shown up unannounced...and left the same way. The idea of Jack hurting Randy or sabotaging his business to get a project contract was sickening. Jack was to all appearances, successful, so why? Without a motive, there was little to go on, unless you counted greed. The historical project would be a lucrative deal for the company awarded the primary contract.

There was only one way to find out if she was right. Taylor dialed the cleaning company. "Good afternoon, First Class Car Care. How can I help you?" a woman asked, her voice bright and chipper. The exact opposite of how Taylor felt, her nerves fragile and ready to snap.

"Hi there. I just found a ticket from your business, and I was hoping you could tell me who it belongs to?"

"Oh dear, I don't know if I can do that," the woman said, suddenly unsure of herself.

Taylor had to somehow convince the woman. "I understand. I don't need the person's address or even the person's full name. I understand privacy rights and all. Initials will be fine, but I would like to return the stub in case they need it for anything. Receipts and taxes go hand in hand." It was a likely story, and the woman's silence gave her hope.

"That's true. And since you're okay with initials, I don't see where it's a problem. What's the ticket number?" *Thank you, Lord.*

"5-3-4-3-4-5-7-7-7. It's dated for *Thursday*."

"That helps. Here it is. The initials of the gentleman who brought his car in for cleaning are JT."

Taylor sucked in a deep breath. Jack Tinsdale. The woman had unknowingly revealed it was a man, which was another confirmation that Jack was still on top of her suspect list. "Thank you so much. I know who it is, and I'll get this receipt back to him." *Via the police.* "You've been such a big help. Have a wonderful day." They hung up and Taylor dropped into the nearest seat to contemplate what she had just learned.

Suspecting Jack was one thing, but obtaining evidence to that effect threw her off kilter. JT didn't exactly tie up her suspicions in a neat tidy bow, but it was certainly enough to call in to the police department and let them decide what to do with the information.

Starting from the first time he showed up to the inn, and when the incidents started happening...right down to the fateful evening where Randy might have died. With the ticket stub in hand, Taylor was certain she would have the police chief's undivided attention.

Chapter Twenty

♥

THE POLICE HAD BEEN more than a little interested in Taylor's theories and the evidence she turned over after they paid her a visit and took her report. She hoped she wasn't raining down misery on an innocent man, but everything pointed to Jack's involvement. And the fact he was married, something one detective let slip, infuriated her. That's where his innocence ended. And if he was guilty of attempted murder, then it would seem Jack had been using her as his unknowing accomplice to gain access to the house. Talk about a sucker punch to the gut. Taylor felt like such a fool.

After updating her parents with her suspicions after the police left, they had been stunned...and supportive. No, *I told you so* concerning Jack. But then, only motive, coincidence, and a ticket stub implicated him. The police investigation would determine the outcome.

The flight back to Raleigh had been quick. She was relieved no one had called with bad updates, which was encouraging. Taylor took it as a good sign, but only once she was back at the hospital with Randy to see him for herself would help assuage any doubts.

Her phone vibrated, and without so much as a glance at the screen she pressed the answer button and then the speaker button, keeping her eyes on the parking lot as she searched to remember where she parked her car. "Hello."

"Taylor Thompson?" The voice was vaguely familiar, but she couldn't place it. Hopefully, it wasn't the hospital calling.

"This is she."

"This is Brian Sanders with the Alaskan Adventures. We spoke a few days ago."

Remorse settled in the pit of her stomach. "Oh, yes, Mr. Sanders. I'm so sorry I missed the interview. I truly appreciate everything you did to give me a chance at the position, but there was an accident, and I couldn't leave. Not me in an accident, a good friend of mine and I had to stay to help. And then everything was so hectic I forgot to email you. I'm so—"

"You can stop apologizing. I know all about the accident. Actually, it's why I'm calling."

The man wasn't making any sense. How in the world would he know? "You do?" Taylor asked.

"Yes. Your mother called our offices, and her call was directed to me. A little unorthodox, mind you, but she certainly didn't want you to miss an opportunity you had your heart set on. Talk about singing your praises."

Good grief. Her mother called. Taylor was mortified and pleased all at once. Perhaps her mom was truly trying to make amends for meddling in her life. "She did?" Her mother never said a word. Not that Taylor had been around much the past couple of days. The fact her mother had gone to such lengths ended all of Taylor's frustration with her interfering ways. Calling the charter company meant her mother had accepted Taylor was returning to San Francisco.

Taylor smiled. The more she thought about it, the cuteness came to mind, and she saw it as another loving...meddling gesture. "I'm sorry, Mr. Sanders. My mother can be interfering."

"I'm glad she called. Otherwise, we might not have known the truth."

"The truth?" Taylor asked, unsure where this was all headed.

"About why you missed the interview. We've seen the accident report and know you pulled an emergency flight to save the man. And we know you had engine failure and still landed the plane. Without injury to anyone on board or to the aircraft. Kudos on a job well done, Ms. Thompson."

Taylor flushed with pleasure under the praise. "Thank you, sir. I did what came naturally, but I must admit I'm feeling good about responding under pressure. A pilot never knows until they face real trouble." She couldn't believe he was calling her to congratulate her on a job well done.

"Which is exactly why we want you on our team."

His words caught her off guard, not at all what she was expecting to hear. "But what about the interview process and the simulated flight test?"

The man chuckled. "Why do we need one of those? You interviewed yourself and passed with flying colors."

Taylor couldn't believe what she was hearing. *The job was hers.* "Thank you so much, Mr. Sanders." She did a little happy dance right there in the parking lot, not caring who saw.

"So, you'll take the job?"

Taylor paused, a moment of doubt clouding her answer. She shoved it aside. This is what she wanted...wasn't it? "Absolutely. And thank you. I should be back in California within a couple of days. If you send me the offer letter, I'll review it right away. And if everything is good, I'm on board. Pun intended." Taylor grinned.

She couldn't wait to tell Sandy and her parents. Maybe she should take her parents out to dinner tomorrow night since it would seem it was all her mother's interfering ways that landed Taylor the job. If Randy was well enough, that is. He came first.

Knowing she loved him and would leave soon was the only reason she could find to explain why she wasn't feeling as thrilled deep down as she should have been about the job offer. It was something to consider later, because right now, getting back to Randy was her priority.

Now that was something that made her heart go pitter patter a little faster with no hesitation.

Taylor pushed open the door to Randy's room and stepped inside. The sound of beeping machines was a stark reminder of the last two days and the worry over his condition. Her prayers had been answered when he finally woke up, and now he needed to get well enough to go home.

He looked up and smiled, her heart doing a somersault in response.

"A welcoming smile is always good in a hospital," she said, returning his warm greeting.

"They're easy when it's you coming to visit and not another nurse wanting to run tests. I'm about tired of being hooked up to this thing," he said, pointing to the IV.

Taylor shook her head. "Then get better, and I'm sure they'll remove it. All in good time."

Randy grimaced. "I'm trying to be patient, but hospitals aren't my thing. You, of all people, should know that."

"I do, but honestly, they aren't anyone's thing…unless you choose to work here." She chuckled, taking a seat in the chair by the window. "I came back to see how you were doing before I head over to Sandy's for the night."

"I'm doing great…thanks to you. Everyone is quick to point out you saved my life."

Taylor felt flush and knew her face had turned beat red. She didn't take compliments well and this was a doozy. "That's what friends are for." She winked, shooting him a grin to bypass the uncomfortable feeling.

"Well, I'm sure glad I've got you on my side. You are, right?" he asked, a sudden frown marring his face.

"Of course. Always."

"So why aren't you back at the inn helping your folks? I mean, I'm in good hands here with the hospital staff and my parents," Randy asked, his gaze intensifying.

It was the loaded question she'd hoped to avoid. "Because you're in here and it's where I need to be. Besides, it turns out my mom was still doing a little matchmaking. I busted her hobbling around on crutches."

Randy shook his head and grinned. "No way."

"Yes way. You know my mom. My parents have been so worried about you. They drove out here Friday but had to go back to take care of the guests. I've been worried too, which is why I had to be here." Telling him the truth would complicate things, but honesty was always best. What if she'd lost him and he never knew the truth? Never knew that she hadn't stopped caring about him. Loving him. Not that her tell all would reveal that much information. Randy's gaze never left her face, his thoughtful expression her undoing. "But enough about that. How are you feeling?" she asked, trying to ease pass the elephant in the room.

. "Well, other than a splitting headache that comes about the time they need to feed in more pain relievers, I'm doing great. I passed multitudes of testing with flying colors and the doctor seems to think I could be out of here in a few days if nothing problematic crops up as an after effect."

"That's wonderful news." Taylor said, comforted by his words and feeling as though she could relax for the first time in days.

"I think the news that you still care about me is even better. We talked about this before, and you shot down my offer of a second chance for us. But I'm still hoping we can be more than friends again. I'm just not sure where you stand with Jack. He was always jealous when you and I dated in high school and now he has you."

Taylor turned away and faced the window. There was so much she needed to explain. "Jack doesn't have me. Never did. But you sound like the jealous one," she teased, turning back to gauge his reaction.

Randy shrugged. "Maybe. Can you blame me? And I don't trust him, especially not with you. He's not good enough for you, Taylor."

The conversation had taken a serious twist, and it was time Randy found out the truth. "You have good reason not to trust him. You'll never believe this, so settle in for a whopper of a story."

Randy quirked an eyebrow up and took a sip of water. "I can't wait to hear and just for the record, I'm relieved you two aren't an item." He settled back against the pillows, looking more relaxed. More at peace with himself...like the Randy she knew and loved.

Taylor pulled the chair closer and told Randy everything. The fact Jack was married, what she suspected initially, the investigation she did on her own after Randy kept insisting that he was pushed, and how it all led to the police sending out a squad car to pick Jack up for questioning. "They might very well have already issued a warrant for his arrest, depending on whether or not he has an alibi for that evening after he dropped me off Thursday night."

Randy shook his head and scowled, the lines across his forehead deepening like caverns. "This is crazy. I mean, we were never friends...but I can't believe Jack would try to kill me over the historical contract. And I can't believe you did all this without telling me. I would have believed you. I hate the idea of you off with him alone, and on my behalf."

"Probably...but then I didn't want to make a false accusation and you would have sided strongly with me simply because it was Jack, and you didn't like him around me. Which is not evidence of guilt. At least not attempted murder, He'll have to answer to his wife for his other antics."

"True." Randy nodded, stifling a yawn.

"I'm just glad you're going to be okay. I hate that Jack might have been using me to get access to the house. Maybe everything would be different if I had seen through his polished facade."

"And maybe nothing would be different. You might have been a means to an end, but without you, a desperate man would have found another way. The way I see it, you saved my life."

"Thank you." Taylor nodded, wanting to believe him. "I need to update my parents on your condition. My plane should be fixed by tomorrow, and then I'll head back to the inn." She still hadn't told him about her new job. *So why was she holding back?*

"About that...if they need to hire someone else to finish the repairs...I'd understand. It's not like I'm in any condition to report back to work soon," Randy said.

"They wouldn't dream of it."

"They have always been super nice to me. Taylor, *is* there any chance for the two of us to reconnect? Knowing what we know about the past...don't we owe it to each other to find out if there could be a future? And you said you still care about me," he added, trying to tip the scales.

Taylor shook her head. It was time to fess up about the job. "Our timing is lousy. As much as I might want to consider the possibility, there's something else I haven't told you yet."

"What's that?" The lines across his forehead deepened.

"I was offered the job with the Alaskan Adventures...and I accepted. They heard about what happened ...the medical flight and the engine failure and my success in landing the plane, courtesy of my mother. I've always felt as though I had something to prove. Living up to my father's ideals and track record hasn't been easy."

"I see about the job. But what do you mean about having to prove something? We talked about this before and you wouldn't explain. Perhaps it's time you trusted me with answers."

Taylor sucked in a deep breath. Nothing locked deep inside would ever truly heal unless it was brought into the light. It would be the freedom to once and for all let go of the past that no longer had the power to embarrass her. "That I'm good enough to be a pilot."

"Again, I don't understand. It makes no sense," Randy said, reaching for her hand.

"No one except Sandy knows what I'm about to tell you."

Taylor went on to explain about the failed simulator test and the doubts she'd had regarding her abilities ever since. Saying the words out loud was like lifting the cloudy veil and letting the light inside her heart for healing. "I've tried so hard to prove to myself, my parents, anyone...that I'm not only qualified to be a pilot, but that I could be an excellent one. Someone people could rely on in an emergency. My dad was a top-notched pilot and I just want him to be proud of me. I'm only telling you all this, so you'll understand why I accepted the job. It's the validation I've needed." Taylor turned to look out the window, finding it easier not to face him.

"Except for the fact you just admitted you recently had that validation...when you flew me here. So why do you still need the job? Not that I agree with your reasoning for wanting it in the first place. This is a good time to reassess your life since you never had anything to prove. Your pilot's license says you're good enough to fly. You were born to be a pilot and help others." Randy's confidence in her had never wavered.

"I don't know. You're right, but it all happened so fast."

"Taylor, sometimes living life means taking a leap of faith. Maybe God is giving us a second chance for a reason. You can still run your own charter business. What about something for the inn? Or medical flight charters?

Anything. There must be an option to combine what you love and share it with the people you love. Just stick around. For us..." The low timber of his voice calmed some of her apprehension, especially knowing everything he said was true.

The problem was that she had already accepted the position...and then Mr. Sanders had gone the extra mile to make her feel as though she would be a valuable member of the team. "I can't. They are expecting me to report in next week to start work."

"It's not too late to change your mind. Promise me you'll think about what I said, Taylor. Think about what the future here could look like. For us." Randy yawned.

Taylor hadn't signed on the dotted line. She didn't even know the terms of the contract...other than it would be an amazing opportunity. "I promise."

Chapter Twenty-One

♥

A FEW DAYS LATER, Randy's parents took him back to their house to keep a close eye on him during the transition back to regular life. Taylor wanted to visit but didn't want to overwhelm Randy and respected their family time together after such a traumatic event. His discharge, however, gave Taylor a full sense of relief...one she hadn't felt since the accident. Or perhaps even long before.

Her whole life had been a series of events, pushing her to higher levels of success. And now, everything was different. Taylor pulled out her suitcase to pack for her return home. With the fuel lines on her plane replaced, the gas drained, and the tank cleaned, there was no reason to delay any longer. Fuel starvation was confirmed, and all the result of deposits in the gas when she refueled on the way to North Carolina. It was an easy repair, but the consequence could have been devastating.

Her computer lay open on the bed, the charter company's employment letter still waiting to be signed. It was an excellent offer. The salary was a tremendous increase, which would be a huge weight off her shoulders when it came to helping her folks with the B&B. The hours were variable but capped weekly. And the bonus package was lucrative with plenty of vacation time. There was no reason not to sign.

Except for one.

Randy.

She had never stopped loving him, and the picture he painted was enticing. Randy believed in her without proof. Believed in them...without proof. He trusted his heart, and he trusted God was giving them another chance. The current path of her future would be more of the same...flying charters...though exciting charters for sure. But she would still be alone. No one to share the stories with, laugh with, or even cry with. No one to step outside of the flying box with to experience more than just the friendly blue skies she loved.

Giving everything up she worked hard for was tempting, but not smart.

Listen to your heart.

It was the same message she heard over and over since the accident. The same message that caused her to admit her feelings. But what if they failed this time around also? History wasn't in their favor. Granted, in the past they were younger, and perhaps not as mature as they assumed. Maybe they simply hadn't been ready and that's where her fears had originated. But that wasn't an excuse she could latch on to any longer.

Taylor finished packing the suitcase and zipped it shut, hoisted it to the ground, and rolled it to the door.

Her mother stood there, tears glistening in her eyes. "I'm so proud of you for getting this job. I knew that if they knew what happened, they would understand. But I hate to see you leave. It's been wonderful having you home, even under all the strained circumstances."

"Why did you call Alaskan Adventures? You were doing everything you could to make me stay longer, and then suddenly did an about face."

"I prayed about it and knew I had been wrong. It's not my life to live...it's yours. I wanted to make amends so that moving forward you wouldn't be upset with me for standing in your way."

"Thank you." Taylor hugged her mother.

"That being said, I would still love to have you back home. Randy or no Randy, I promise," her mother said, crossing her heart.

Taylor shook her head. "I'm so confused."

"About?"

"Whether or not to go. Randy is a factor...the biggest factor truth be told." She couldn't believe she was admitting as much to her mother.

"Then stay. There will be other jobs. You're good at what you do, and any company would be lucky to have you." It was the same message Randy and her father continually tried to tell her.

Taylor let out a deep breath. Her mother was right. It was a big step and a gigantic risk, but Randy was at the end of the road if she gave them another chance.

"Thanks, Mom." Taylor closed her laptop and slid it in the case. She hugged her mother again, delaying the inevitable for as long as possible. A horn sounded from outside the cabin. "That's dad. I've got to go. I just think it's too late to change my mind since I told the company yes. It wouldn't be right to just walk away without good reason."

Her mother shrugged, a hint of sadness in her eyes. "It's never too late, dear. In life or love. Just remember that." *Words of wisdom.*

Taylor brushed back the tears that threatened to fall. "I love you, Mom. I'm so glad you are on the mend and doing well."

"Thank you, dear. And thanks for helping us when we really needed you. And again, I'm truly sorry for my meddling ways."

"You're welcome and you're forgiven. Say no more. It's because you love me and want what you think is best for me. There's nothing wrong with that." It was true, and she had forgiven her parents for the subterfuge.

"But about what you want. Think carefully. You said Randy is the biggest part of the picture and the decision. You've been given a second chance with him, which might not come around again. What do you feel in your heart? Can you find peace, love, and joy in Alaska with someone else? Because that is what's most important. Not a job. Loving what you do is important, but it's not your whole life. Relationships and family are important. There must be a balance."

"I wish I knew the answer. I'll have plenty of time to think about it on the way home." Taylor smiled, trying to find a joy she wasn't experiencing.

Taylor lugged her suitcase down the hall and out the front door. Her father joined her, taking the suitcase and putting it in the truck's bed. He was taking her to the local airport where she would catch a flight back to Raleigh to pick up her plane and head west.

"Ready to go?" he asked when he spotted her coming out the door.

She nodded. "Ready as I'll ever be, I guess."

Her father quirked one eyebrow up and frowned but didn't say a word. Taylor waved at her mother, as she stood on the porch to watch her leave.

"She'll get over you leaving. Don't worry. The question is, will you?" her father asked, nailing the million-dollar question on the head.

"I wish I knew. Mom keeps asking me the same thing. I agreed to work for the charter company, and I feel as though I owe them."

"You agreed before you knew all the terms." Her father pulled away from the curb and headed down the long driveway.

"But the terms are good. Better than expected," Taylor countered.

"I'm not talking about the contractual terms."

"Then what?" she asked, turning to face him.

"The terms of your heart. Those are more important than anything else. You're in love with Randy...still. I'm not blind."

"It's true. I've admitted as much, but what—"

"There is no but, sweetheart. God is giving the two of you a second chance to work things out. Don't you think you owe it to the both of you to have that chance? Work is work, but it's not the end all for life. Your faith in God and who you choose to share your life with far outweigh any job."

Her father's comment echoed her mothers, but this time the words found their mark.

Taylor's heart.

Work wasn't meant to run her entire life...and it's not like she didn't have options. And like everyone kept telling her...she hadn't signed the contract. Maybe she'd known all along she couldn't sign it and that's why she hesitated in the first place? What if leaving Moonridge would be the biggest mistake of her life?

"Stop the truck, Dad."

Her father pulled over to the side of the road. "What is it? Did you forget something?"

Taylor grinned. "I did. Randy." Tears of joy ran unchecked down her face, the enormity of the decision hitting home.

Her father covered her hand in his and squeezed. "That a girl."

"Any chance I can work for you at the B&B?" she asked, recalling Randy's suggestions and knowing the opportunity to put everything together that she loved was not an opportunity to be missed. It would be a huge change, but she believed in herself...and in Randy.

"I would love it, but sweetheart, business isn't what it once was. Your mother, of course, would overlook the practical side of things and be thrilled."

"But what if I could help revitalize the inn? Randy mentioned some things I think would work if you're willing to let me try." It really would be best all the way around, but if her father didn't agree, Taylor would still stay in Moonridge and go it alone on the business plan she was formulating in her head.

"I'm listening."

"What if I got Sandy to help me redesign the website, and we set up a wedding event venue? Something to specifically attract folks to book here that they aren't getting at the competition. And I could offer charter flights to all the guests if needed. Really go after a select clientele.

This would be my charter company, with my own hours and schedule." The more she verbalized the plan, the more excited she got about it.

"It's a great idea but are you sure that's what you would want to do?" her father asked, pulling up to the front of the house.

"I am. And the big plus is that I can offer emergency medical flights as a backup to what the area currently offers. There seems to be a need."

"I love that idea even more. Helping others. The B&B might do more than survive with you on our team." He went around the truck and pulled her suitcase out.

"It might just work, and anything worth having is worth going the distance to get it. Including my relationship with Randy."

"That's my girl. Your mother will be over the moon." Her father hugged her tight.

"Then let's go tell her," Taylor said, ready to set her new future in motion.

Chapter Twenty-Two

♥

It went without saying that her mother was overjoyed she was moving back home to work with them, but more than that, she wanted Taylor to be happy. Her mother wanted her to have the kind of love that transcended time and carried a couple through the highs and lows of life.

The kind of love she wanted with Randy.

Taylor had called the charter company with her regrets, put in her notice at her current job, and flown home to pack up her things. She grinned as the last of the boxes were taped shut and labeled, ready to be loaded into her plane. There were three hours left until she was scheduled to take off, and all that was left to do was turn in her keys to the apartment.

With one last look around the place, she shut the door. A chapter in her life was closing and a new one was beginning. And Taylor trusted God would help her sort out what the new beginning would look like, but she was fully committed to making her life one filled with peace, joy....and love.

Randy was due back to work this week, and she hadn't spoken to him since she left, wanting to have everything final. Taylor wanted everything in place to not only show her commitment to them as a couple, but for her life in North Carolina. The time was well spent as she put together a business plan and worked with Sandy on the website. Best of all, Sandy was moving to Moonridge and was partnering with Taylor in the new charter company...Heart to Heart.

Sandy's nursing talents would be amazing for any medical airlifts, her customer service and organizational skills a must for charter flights, and a website designer extraordinaire. Her multi-talented friend would be a huge asset to the business.

It would be interesting to see where her friend and Dane ended up, though Sandy declared her decision to work with Taylor had nothing to do with him. And it was probably true, but it also didn't mean it couldn't be viewed as a positive aspect of the upcoming changes.

Her parents and Sandy had been sworn to silence thus far about the business and Taylor's decision to move home. The old saying...actions speak louder than words...well that was the plan Taylor put in place to let Randy in on what was happening. It hadn't taken long for her to figure out a way to make the moment special. Something big enough that all but shouted *I love you*, so he would understand...and believe.

Her mother, of course, wanted Taylor to move into one of the cabins, but she wasn't interested in going to that extreme. She still wanted some autonomy from her parents. Her father suggested she buy a house in town, something close enough to make quick airlift flights when needed. He was right of course.

She discovered a moderately sized home on the outskirts of town that fell under the historic designation because once upon a time the President of the United States stayed there on a weekend getaway. It had been owned by the first family for two generations, but had eventually been sold, the family staying in much bigger, more posh places after success had catapulted the family into the limelight.

And it was perfect for what Taylor needed. There was much work to be done, but it fit her budget and had plenty of room to run a business from one of the extra bedrooms. It would also be big enough to accommodate a family should things work out the way she planned.

Taylor set up the inspection in two days' time. A time for which she planned to meet with the local construction company approved by the town council for historical renovations.

Renovations by Design.

Randy.

Two days later, Taylor met the realtor and the inspector at the house. She moved through the home, itemizing what she felt the place needed. After checking her watch for the hundredth time, she realized it was finally time for her next appointment. She moved to the living room, pacing as she watched through the front window for Randy's arrival. Not that he had any idea who he was meeting since the appointment was with a rep from Heart to Heart.

Randy pulled into the driveway, right on time. Taylor steeled herself, prepared for the worst and hoping for the best as he stepped out of the truck. He looked good. *Fantastic.* It was hard to believe a week and a half ago he'd been in a coma. It was as though he'd never missed a step. Taylor met him at the door, pulling it wide open.

His confused expression was endearing. "Taylor? I thought you were in California?"

She grinned. "Good morning. And to answer your question, I was. Now I'm here." She'd waited for this moment for eight years and was savoring the moment, praying it would go well.

"But I'm supposed to meet with the owner of a company called Heart to Heart."

Taylor nodded. "So, you are. That's me. I own Heart to Heart. Or well…Sandy and I own the company together."

"Sandy? I don't understand. Are you moving here?" he asked.

"Moved. I'm under contract for this house, and I'm having the inspections done today. I was hoping you could give me a quote for some of the renovations I've got planned."

"This is great news. But can I ask why you moved back to Moonridge?" His gaze held hers, searching for the truth.

"Well, you put the bug in my ear about starting up my own charter company, and I feel it was a capital idea. Heart to Heart will start charter flights next month for the inn, specializing in wedding venues. More importantly, I'll sign up as a medical rescue flight option for emergency services. There's simply not enough available around here in this remote area of the mountains."

Randy's smile was like a ray of sunshine. "Guess that idea comes from me as well. Do I get a commission?" he teased.

"No, but I'm giving you first dibs on the renovations of this house."

"You still trust me?" he asked, running a hand through his hair, as though he were still unsure of where this was headed. Something she needed to make crystal clear.

Taylor closed the distance between them. "Of course. It only appeared you were accident prone. Now we know you're not."

"I still can't believe Jack would do something to such an extreme," Randy said, shaking his head.

"According to my father, Jack's gambling debts are astronomical. It'll be a long time before he needs to worry about money since prison doesn't offer many gambling venues." His poor wife was left to clean-up the mess he'd made of their affairs, but Taylor was proud of the woman for trying.

"I agree. Attempted murder carries a hefty sentence. So why me for this place?" Randy asked.

"Well, you are the historical society's preferential choice." Taylor took another step closer, until they were standing toe to toe.

"I see. Is that the only reason?" he asked, his voice low and urgent.

Her heart raced, knowing it was time to let Randy in on her little secret. "No. I also figured you would be the best judge of what needs to be done in a house that one day you might call your own." She reached out to touch his arm, so there was no mistaking what she meant.

Randy's eyes widened; his head cocked to one side. "Say that again."

"You heard me." Taylor grinned. "Seeing as I'm back in town, and that, I seem to remember a certain guy asking me for a second chance. I reckon I'm saying yes to a relationship between us...if you still want one."

Randy pulled her into his embrace. "Of course, I want one. But what about your job in Alaska?"

"I told them no. My heart is here...with you. I need to believe in myself and in us. I don't want any regrets down the road for not listening to my heart. A job is a job...but love...is everything."

"Amen to that," he said, lowering his head and kissing her. Finally. It was like coming home to her happy place.

"Excuse me, you two," Sandy said, coming into the living room.

Randy and Taylor jumped apart.

"I didn't know you were coming today," Taylor said.

Sandy laughed. "Clearly. I wanted to sign the lease on the new apartment."

"You're moving here too?" Randy asked, looking back and forth between her and Sandy.

"Yup. After all, I own half of Heart to Heart, so where better to live?"

Randy shook his head. "Wow. You two are something else. I can't believe you set all this up and I didn't know a thing. Wait till I tell Dane. Or does he already know? That man is head over heels for you already."

"I feel the same way about him, but I would prefer it if you let me do the telling. I mean, look at you two. If keeping Heart to Heart a secret gets me kissed like that, I'm all in." Sandy grinned, moving further into the living room.

The three of them laughed, the sound like warmth in a home where memories longed to be made. *Their memories.*

"I told you Sandy was my partner. I do the flying and she does just about everything else. I got the easy end of the deal."

"Don't let her fool you. That woman spends more time with her plane keeping it in tip top shape than anyone

I know. I would bet maintenance occupies more hours than flying.”

“Well, hopefully I can cut into that time.”

“Consider my time cut,” Taylor said, grinning at Randy.

Epilogue

♥

THE LAST TWO MONTHS had been the absolute busiest times of Taylor's life. *And the best.* Between helping her parents modernized the cabins and the inn with the new event venue in mind, getting Heart to Heart up and running, moving in her place, and helping Sandy move in and get settled at her apartment, there didn't seem to be much time for anything else. But she'd made time.

For Randy.

He was worth the never-ending feeling they wouldn't have everything done in time for the grand re-opening of the Great Smoky Mountain Hideaway. And all in time to coincide with the Fall into Winter Festival that kicked off the winter season in Moonridge. Business had been picking up slowly, but now, with the new website, reservations were coming in from all over the country. And to her relief, the fly-in option was a huge success.

Sandy had transferred to the nearest hospital and worked part time. She and Dane were quite the item, and Taylor suspected things were getting quite serious between them.

And as a bonus, Taylor had signed on for a quarterly flight to remote areas of the world to bring medical supplies to communities. And Sandy would go with her to offer free health care to those in need. Taylor's dream of flying around the world was finally coming true. Love, peace, and joy...blessings made available through a love of God and her faith.

Glancing around the room, she was pleased with the results of the grand re-opening. Every detail of the party was perfect. The music played, people danced, and friends, family, past guests, and current guests alike were having a lovely time.

Taylor let out a deep breath of relief. Everything had gone off without a hitch, thanks to the team effort of everyone's help along the way. Now was the time to enjoy the fruits of their labor.

Except there was one last surprise in store for the guests, one that had Taylor more than a little nervous. Or maybe it was more like giddy with excitement. She checked her watch, noting the time was at hand for her plan to kick into gear.

"Taylor, dear. Have you seen your father?" her mother asked.

Yes. "Sorry, mom. I haven't. I will tell him you're looking for him if I see him." Her father was a huge part of the last piece of her hidden agenda.

"He's been gone for at least a half an hour. Maybe I should go look for him," her mother said, a worried frown marring her face.

"I'm sure he's fine. Relax. Enjoy the party." It wouldn't do to worry her mom when Taylor knew her father was on an errand for her.

"But he's supposed to make the toast," she insisted.

"I'm sure he'll be here soon. I know he's stressed over what to say and has written a lovely speech to thank everyone." Taylor knew exactly when her father would be back, as he and his pilot friend were on a mission.

"Well, okay. I'll give him ten more minutes and then I'll have to say something on his behalf. Can't have anyone leave without a hearty thank you for all they've done and meant to us. This has been such a wonderful party, and we are so blessed to have such care and love come back to us after all these years of being open for business."

"Trust me, it'll be fine. Look, there's Randy. I need to tell him something." Actually, she needed to be with him *before* the show started. "Got to run, Mother."

"But—"

Taylor didn't hear a word as she crossed the room to Randy's side. "Having fun?"

"Absolutely. You really pulled everything together for your folks. Your love shows for them in everything you do."

"I've always heard show, don't tell." Taylor laughed. And this time, she was doing the *show don't tell* in grand style.

"Then show me." Randy grinned as he kissed her.

Taylor pulled back. "Oh, I'll show you all right, mister." It was her turn to shoot him a satisfied smile.

"What do you—"

"Excuse me, Taylor. Some guests outside are claiming your dad and another guy have the Piper fired up and ready for takeoff at the end of the runway," Dane said, a worried look on his face.

"No way. Not yet." Taylor grabbed Randy by the arm and propelled him forward. Her father was a couple of minutes ahead of schedule, but Taylor knew how to roll with this change in plan. "Hey, everyone. We should all go outside and join the others. Hurry, scurry," she said, pulling Randy out the door.

"But Taylor, what about your fath—" her mother said, stopping her.

"Come on, Mother. It'll be fine, and you won't want to miss this. Trust me," Taylor said.

"Taylor Lynn, what's going on?" her mother demanded, a frown marring her expression.

Taylor grinned. "Come with us, and you'll see."

They moved to the front yard just as her father became airborne.

"Is that your father flying your plane?" her mother asked, her voice rising with panic.

"It is."

"What in heaven's name is the old fool doing?" Her mother's favorite expression when she didn't agree with her father's decisions, but Taylor knew it was born of love laced with a dose of worry.

"Exactly what he should be doing," Taylor said, pulling Randy toward the front of the crowd for a bird's-eye view.

"You don't seem too upset considering you don't let anyone fly your plane," Randy said.

"You're forgetting it was his plane before mine. If anyone else should be trusted to fly her…it's my father. Besides, he's doing it for a good cause." Taylor winked, her cheeks aching as her smile broadened.

Several people pointed to the plane as it made a turn back toward them.

"What's the red tail? Is the plane leaking something?" her mother asked, her voice rising in panic.

"No, everything's fine. Don't worry," Taylor said, trying not to panic the group. She hadn't considered her mother's reaction, or overreaction in this case.

As her father drew closer, it became obvious the plane wasn't leaking anything. It was flying a banner. Soon, the words became visible to everyone in the crowd, the white letters against the rose-red backdrop unmistakable.

I LOVE YOU, RANDY. WILL YOU MARRY ME?

Taylor never took her eyes off Randy. She knew the second the words registered. He turned to her and grinned, pulling her close. With a shake of his head, his gaze followed the plane until it disappeared out of sight past the house. Everyone was silent, and Taylor sensed all eyes were on her and Randy. She was putting everything on the line, including her heart, for everyone to see. But the only one that mattered was Randy.

And he had yet to answer.

"Randy?" she asked, suddenly more nervous than she had ever been in her life.

"Sorry, you took me off guard. Of course, I'll marry you. I'm yours always and forever because I love you too. But—" he said, drawing back a step.

She hadn't expected a *but* in the answer. "What?" she asked, her mouth dry.

Randy reached into his pocket and then dropped to one knee. "Will *you* marry me?"

"You have a ring?" she gasped, her voice like a squeaky mouse. Randy held out a beautiful diamond with aquamarines all around it. Unique and stunning, Taylor brushed back the tears that fell.

"Yes, I was planning on asking you today...after your father gave his speech. Seems you beat me to a proposal. So, will you? Marry me, that is. Seeing as I've already agreed to marry you, I'm hoping you'll say yes," he teased.

"Yes. Yes. Yes." Taylor said, throwing her arms around his neck and pulling him close for a kiss. "I can't believe you were going to ask me today."

With his forehead against hers, his smile was for her and her alone. "Except you always seem to be one step ahead of me."

"Not anymore. We'll be together. Side by side, as God intended. I promise."

"I like that promise. Do you like the ring?"

"It's the most beautiful ring in the world," she beamed.

"Good. I had it designed especially for you. The aquas are the sky and the diamond in the middle is you. The light of my life. I love you, Taylor."

"I love you, too." They kissed again, and everyone around them erupted into cheers.

Her father's friend, Steve, had agreed to let her father fly under his control and licensing, and her dad had been over the moon with the mission. It was almost like the honor of walking his daughter down the aisle. *Only the precursor.*

He landed the plane and joined in the celebration, her mother having a thing or two to say about his adventure. Her dad's thank you speech went off without a hitch.

And as for her mother, well, she was already planning the grandchildren.

Also By Elsie Davis

Sweet, Clean and Wholesome Stories...with a Happily-Ever-After Guarantee!

Great Smoky Mountain Getaways

(Christian Inspirational – Women's Fiction Romances)

Juliet's Journey to Love

Poppy's Path to Love

Rachel's Road to Love

Taylor's Trek to Love

Grace's Getaway to Love – 2024

Dixie's Detour to Love – 2025

Angel's Adventure to Love – 2025

Crossroads Creek Cowboys

(Christian Inspirational Romances)

The Heart of a Cowboy

The Help of a Cowboy

The Return of a Cowboy

The Care of a Cowboy

The Dream of a Cowboy – 2024

The Life of a Cowboy – 2025

The Tears of a Cowboy – 2025

Holidays in Hallbrook
(Sweet Romance Series for Holidays Throughout the
Year)
**Welcome to Hallbrook, New Hampshire. A small-town
filled with the unexpected, lots of love, and of course, a
beloved dog to ramp up the excitement.**
Love & Order (Labor Day)
Love & Family (Thanksgiving)
Love & Peace (Christmas)
Love & Chocolate (Valentine's Day)

Love & Hope (Mother's Day)
Love & Liberty (Independence Day)
Love & Honor (Veteran's Day)
Love & Joy (Easter)
Love & Adventure (Father's Day)

Crestfield Inn Romances

If you like special kinds of soulmates, a splash of the supernatural, and wholesome relationships, you'll adore this sweet bit of fun filled with romance and mystery.

Turning Back Time

Turning Up Roses

Turning Down Pie

Celebrity Corgi Romance

(Standalone Sweet Romance)

If you like light mystery mixed in with your happily-ever-after, you'll enjoy this second-chance romance and the race to save an adorable Corgi.

Digging the Driver

Gold Coast Retrievers

(Sweet Romance)

Special Golden Retrievers help their humans solve mysteries, save lives, and even find love...

Defending Dakota

Trinity River

(Sweet Western Romance)

Ranchers and farmers depend on the Trinity River for water, but when a secret conglomerate starts buying up property by fair means or foul, it's time for the landowners of Tumble County to fight back—Texas style. But what they don't count on, is finding love in the process.

Back in the Rancher's Arms

Small Town, Big Secrets

Sundancer's Legacy – 9 Book series

Sundancer's Star – Available Now

Sundancer's Joy – 2024

Sundancer's Heart – 2024

2025/2026

Sundancer's Majesty

Sundancer's Miracle

Sundancer's Glory

Sundancer's Kiss

Sundancer's Moon

Sundancer's Splendor

About The Author

Elsie Davis is a *USA Today and International Bestselling Author* of over 30 sweet, clean, and wholesome romances, and a member of the ACFW. She discovered the world of Happily-Ever-After romance at the age of twelve when she began avidly reading Barbara Cartland, the Queen of Romance, and has been hooked ever since. After building her dream log home on top of a small mountain, she turned her attention to do what she loves most, writing. Elsie writes sweet Contemporary Romance and Contemporary Christian Romance from her heart...hoping to share a little love in a big world.

When she's not writing, she can be found birding, kayaking, camping, fishing, playing disc golf, and taking nature walks—hoping to spot wildlife. Basically, she loves all things outdoors, EXCEPT cold weather. She and her husband are avid Caribbean cruisers, but Elsie's favorite vacation was their cruise to Alaska. (In spite of the cold!) Indoors, she enjoys a toasty fire, and of course, a great romance with a guaranteed Happily-Ever-After.

https://www.elsiedavishea.com